PRETTY FIERCE

PRETTY FIERCE

KIERAN SCOTT

sourcebooks
fire

Published by Sourcebooks Fire, an imprint of Sourcebooks, Inc.
P.O. Box 4410, Naperville, Illinois 60567-4410
(630) 961-3900
Fax: (630) 961-2168
www.sourcebooks.com

Library of Congress Cataloging-in-Publication data is on file with the publisher.

Source of Production: Versa Press, East Peoria, Illinois, United States
Date of Production: February 2017
Run Number: 5008690

Printed and bound in the United States of America.
VP 10 9 8 7 6 5 4 3 2 1

For my mom, who would've really loved this book.

18 MONTHS AGO

"AND THE CHAMPION GOES DOWN!"

I laid down my cards and raised my fists in the air. Yes, this was a bit juvenile, but I could count on one hand the number of times I'd beaten my mother at any game—chess, UNO, hangman, Monopoly (we had travel versions of every game ever made)—so I decided to give myself a pass. My mother didn't react, however. When I looked up from the table, she was staring at the hotel room door. My heart gave a tiny squeeze.

"Mom?"

She refocused, her dark eyes flitting to me, then the table. "Wait, what? You won? How did that happen?"

The joking tone of her voice was forced. Her eyes found the digital clock on the bedside table. It was 4:22 p.m. She seemed confused by this. And she was too fidgety. Something was wrong. I chose to ignore this. Call it self-preservation.

Because maybe she was still mad at me for what I'd said before we'd left for Oaxaca. That I didn't want this life anymore. That I wanted to be normal. Which, while it was somewhat true,

I'd said it in a fit of emotion after my father had come home four days late from a job and looking like someone had mistaken his face for a piñata. I never would have said it out loud if I'd had time to think.

Because I loved my parents. And they loved our life. We were a unit. A family. We were all we had. I would never turn my back on them. She had to know that.

"It happened when you weren't looking." I cocked my head to one side and knit my brow, hoping to keep the playful vibe going. "Maybe it's that you're getting so old."

My mother lifted one finger. "Watch yourself, mija. I eat little girls like you for breakfast."

She gathered the cards, the gold locket she always wore glinting in the meager light that slipped through the crack in the drawn curtains. I sat back and took a pretzel from the bag I'd been gradually decimating for the last half hour. When I was little—two or three—my mom used to say that to me all the time, then pretend to devour my stomach, showering my skin with kisses and tickling me with her nose. I relaxed now, a warm feeling of security coming over me. Everything was fine. I knew it was fine. When was it ever not fine?

There was a click outside the door. I heard the catch in her throat.

"Mom? Is everything okay?" I asked finally.

I didn't usually question my parents. Especially not when we were in the middle of a job. But I'd never seen her act like this before. Elena Thompson was unshakable. As far as I knew, she'd never broken a sweat in her life. And right now, the hands that each held one half a deck of cards were trembling.

She put the cards down and wiped her palms on her hips, leaving finger-shaped trails on her otherwise pristine black pants.

"Yes, of course. Everything's fine. Your turn to shuffle."

I was reaching for the cards when the Batphone let out an unfamiliar peel. We both stopped breathing. "The Batphone" was our cutesy name for the untraceable cell we brought with us everywhere. The cell that was only supposed to be used when something went very, very wrong. I'd never heard it ring until now.

My mother's olive skin went gray. She stood up and froze. The phone peeled again.

"Mom?" I said.

She picked it up. Looked at the screen. Her eyelids fluttered.

"Mom?" I said again, though this time my voice sounded nothing like my own.

That was when the gunshots rang out.

chapter 1
KAIA

I DIDN'T SEE THE TWO-BY-FOUR COMING. I'D REGISTERED THE CREAK of the floorboards a breath before the bastard knocked me unconscious. Or bastards. It was hard to tell how many there were, what with my eyes still struggling to focus as I slowly came to.

"Where is she?"

A man's breath was hot against my face, smelling of pickles and tobacco. He ran the tip of a blade along my cheekbone, leaving a trail of puncture marks, each stinging in its own special way. My forehead throbbed from the initial blow that had knocked me out, and my eyes felt like one hard shake would pop them from their sockets and send them rolling across the floor. Hard to believe that a couple of hours ago I was debating whether or not to let Chelsea Franks switch lockers with me so she could be closer to her boyfriend. I'd been leaning toward no, because hey, maybe if she couldn't assert her independence I'd assert it for her. But now, here I was, tied to a chair with my arms twisted uncomfortably behind me, taunted by some assface who was clearly out for blood.

But *was* it a couple of hours ago? How long had I actually been unconscious? The sun seemed weak behind the pink, flowered curtains of Bess and Henry's living room, but it had been cloudy all day.

And where were Henry and Bess anyway? They were always here when I got home from school. My fingers curled into sweaty fists. If this motherfucker had done anything to hurt my pseudoparentals, he was going to regret it.

"Tell me where she is," he whispered, corkscrewing the tip of the blade near the corner of my mouth, as if trying to give me a dimple, "and I'll make it quick."

Tears stung my eyes, but I refused to let them fall. The man had a German accent, pale skin, and greasy blond hair, plus a twitchy demeanor that spoke of someone who was never quite sure where he stood. Why the hell was he here? Did this have something to do with the Hamburg job? We'd barely stayed in town three days. *Simple*, my dad had said. *In and out.* Did someone know we had been there—what my parents had done—and sent this guy after me? Who, exactly, was I dealing with?

I tugged at the binds on my wrists and they pulled apart slightly. *Eureka.* Sometimes being five feet nothing with baby cheeks and big blue eyes was a plus. People mistook me for a weak little girl. And when people underestimated me, I usually managed to take advantage. I bent my head forward and squeezed out a tear.

"I don't know what you're talking about," I whimpered.

"Yes, you do, you little bitch!"

My face exploded as the man backhanded me across the cheek. The rickety dining chair he'd tied me to fell sideways, and my shoulder collided with the floor. I heard a crack, and the hold on my wrists loosened. One of the spindles on the back of the chair had splintered. My heart flipped with excitement. I curled my chin toward my chest, pretending to sob, and worked my wrists until they were entirely free.

The guy hit the ground in front of me, kneeling to bring his face close to mine. I could see a fleck of blackish-green lodged between two teeth.

"You know where your mother is hiding, Kaia. So why don't you make this easier on the both of us and simply tell me?"

I looked into his blue eyes and started to laugh. I tried to hold it in, but I couldn't help it. He clearly believed what he was saying, which made the situation that much funnier. As I struggled to catch my breath, the guy sat back, blatantly surprised.

"That's what this is about?" I spat, still playing possum on the floor. "My mother? My mother is dead, you idiot. She's been dead for more than a year!"

His ugly, pockmarked face twisted into a condescending smile. "That's where you're wrong, *schnuckelchen*," he said, rising to his feet. In the waning light, his fair eyebrows disappeared, giving him the look of a very angry, very nasty, newborn baby. "Your mama is alive and well and living the high life while you rot in this waste of a town with only those pathetic geriatrics to protect you."

He was lying. Obviously he was lying. If my mother were alive, she never would have left me to get out of Oaxaca last year by myself—not by choice. If my mother were alive and she'd been *forced* to run, she would still have come to get me months ago. We'd be off in Brazil or Morocco or South Africa together, planning our next move, trying to find out what had happened to my father. Why he'd never shown up to do the job he'd been paid so generously to do. But none of that was any of this guy's business, so I wouldn't bother trying to talk him out of his delusions. He had no idea the condition my mother had been in the last time I'd seen her. That was also no business of his. And it was something I preferred not to think about. I focused, instead, on the more pressing matter.

"How did you find me?"

His thin lips curled into a sneer. "Word is out, *liebling.* You should thank me because I'm going to make your death nice and quick. Others will be coming for you and they won't be as kind as I intend to be."

Others? The very word sent a spiral of fear down my spine.

"What did you do to Henry and Bess?" I demanded.

Slowly, the visitor walked past me, slipping the side of his knife across the placket of his gray pinstriped jacket over and over again. My blood left tiny red hash marks in the fabric. He came to a stop behind my chair.

"To who? Those trolls you call protectors? I'm sure they'll find their bodies before the end of the month."

A real sob welled in my throat. "You sonofa—"

He grabbed me by the hair. Before he could bring the knife to my neck, I drew my arms forward, then yanked my elbows back as hard as I could into his gut. His knife hit the floorboards as he doubled over and I kicked it away. He was as good as dead, but knives were not my style. I was a gun girl, born and raised. I yanked the shotgun off the mantel—the one Henry had told me he always kept loaded in case of emergency—turned around, and whacked the guy across the chin with the side of the stock so hard even I saw stars. I was going to have to thank Bess for making me keep up the kickboxing training—for keeping me strong. If I ever saw her again.

Please let this guy be lying about what he's done to them. Henry and Bess had become my family over the last year and a half. They were the only family I had left. I couldn't lose anyone else. I just couldn't.

The impact from my blow had laid the German out, and I brought my foot down on his neck, choking off his air supply.

Shotguns leave a serious mess, and they can be painful as hell to fire, but you can load the shell from the magazine into the chamber with one hand. *Click clack.* It's pretty badass. I aimed the gun at his face and looked down the sight line at the man's quivering, bloody upper lip.

"Please, kid," he rasped. "Please. I'm only doing my job."

"Not anymore," I said.

See? Badass.

But then I started to sweat. My throat tightened, and my vision went fuzzy. I didn't want to do this. Not really. Not

again. But I had to. If I didn't kill him, he was most definitely
going to kill me.

I had this sudden, vivid memory of my uncle Marco frying
ants with a magnifying glass when I was about five. When I'd
burst into tears, he'd looked over his shoulder at me, his glass
eye glinting, and sneered. *"Survival of the fittest, baby."*

"Please kid," the guy choked out now. "Please."

I clenched my teeth. My finger twitched on the trigger.
Before I ended him, I needed to ask him who'd sent him here.
It was what my parents would have done.

"Kaia?"

I blinked. The screen door creaked open, and Oliver
was there, staring. Oliver Lange. My boyfriend. His unruly
blond curls were slicked back with water from his postpractice
shower, and his solid soccer bod practically filled the doorway.
Oliver was the love of my life. The only person left on this
godforsaken earth who gave two shits about me.

"What're you doing?"

He looked, understandably, like he was about to throw
up, and suddenly I was reliving, in vivid detail, the day just
over a year ago when Oliver and I had met. I'd dropped my
books all over the floor in front of my locker when Oliver's
soccer ball had hit my shoulder—an accident that felt like
the icing on the crapcake that was my life. It was my second
week at South Charleston High School—the first normal
school I'd ever been to, and hardly anyone had said a word
to me. I'd spent every night for three months not sleeping,

searching the Internet for any sign of my parents, waiting for a text or a call or an email, and afraid of the nightmares I had whenever I closed my eyes. I was so exhausted that when my books hit the floor, I'd almost lost it. Yes, I'd almost cried over spilled books.

But then Oliver was there, helping to gather up my things, looking directly into my eyes. And unbelievably, what I'd seen there was understanding.

"Hey," he said. "It's gonna be okay."

"Is it?" I asked.

"I'm Oliver," he said.

"I'm Kaia," I replied.

He offered his hand to shake, and when our fingers touched, I knew nothing would ever be the same.

"Kaia?" Oliver said again in the here. In the now.

I blinked.

Behind him, a black SUV careened around the corner into view. No plates. It didn't belong here. We were about to have more company. And Oliver was in their line of fire.

No. Hot desperation welled inside my chest. *Not Oliver.*

He was everything good and pure in this world. Broken, yes. But to me that made him all the more perfect. And he loved me. Almost every single detail I'd told him about myself had been a lie, except for the fact that I loved him too. That was 100 percent true. And I wasn't about to let him die.

I flipped the gun around, brought the butt down in the center of Picklebreath's forehead, and snatched my canvas backpack from the floor. My eyes lit on the German's duffel, tossed carelessly next to the front entry.

"Grab his bag," I ordered Oliver.

"What?"

I groaned, leaned past him, and picked it up myself. Brakes squealed outside.

"Get inside!" I shouted to Oliver as I grabbed his arm and dragged him into the house.

"What the hell is going on?"

"Oliver, I swear I will explain everything!" I shoved him ahead of me, through the kitchen toward the back door. There was blood all over the floor—Betty and Henry's blood—and he slipped in it as he reached for the handle. I swallowed hard and held my breath to keep from throwing up. Outside, a second set of brakes screeched, and a car door popped, then another, then another. "Please! Just run!"

chapter 2

OLIVER

My HEART WAS THUDDING SO HARD IT FELT AS IF IT WAS BEING SHOT with a nail gun over and over and over again as Kaia threw two bags and her gun—her *gun*—into the backseat of her grandfather's truck. They clattered against one of her skateboards. I slammed the door, shaking, and hadn't even managed to touch the seat belt when she shoved the car into first and shot forward. She was about to drive us right through the door of the detached garage.

"Kaia, are you freaking crazy?"

Shifting through gears like a NASCAR pro, she cut the wheel at the last second, and we slammed onto the dirt, then bucked over some uneven slabs of broken concrete. The wheels crushed the plastic kiddie chairs in the neighbors' backyard, and someone screamed, but Kaia gunned it. I closed my eyes, grabbed the handle above the door, and held my breath as we raced toward Caroline Street, flying over the curb and onto the road. Thankfully there were no cars in sight.

"Are you okay?" Kaia asked me, her eyes on the rearview mirror.

There was a massive lump on her forehead—yellow and purple around the edges—and she was bleeding. Not a lot, but still. My gut clenched with a mixture of terror and anger and fear—a combination I only ever experienced when my foster father made his unscheduled appearances at our backdoor—and I felt the insatiable need to punch something. Had that squirrelly-looking guy back at her house done this to her? And whose blood was all over the kitchen floor?

Kaia wrenched the wheel to the left, and the tires squealed. It made no sense whatsoever, but she looked kind of...excited.

"What the fuck is going on?" I asked.

I don't usually swear, but extreme situations call for extreme language. Like when you walk into your girlfriend's house to find her staring down the front sight of a shotgun with her foot pressed against some guy's jugular. Now we were flying down a local road at sixty miles an hour, and I had blood all over my shoes—my only good shoes—and no clue where we were headed. If that weren't disturbing enough, the sight of Kaia wielding said shotgun had kind of turned me on.

"I don't know," she said. "But we have to get out of here."

There was a sudden noise, like a car backfiring, and my side-view mirror shattered.

"Shit!" Kaia shouted.

She jammed the wheel to the right, taking the ramp onto Route 17 at the last second, nearly flattening a twenty-five-miles-per-hour sign in the process.

"What the hell was that?" I demanded.

"They're shooting at us."

She said this calmly, leaning forward over the wheel.

"Shooting?" My voice cracked in a very unmanly way as I slid down in the seat until my knees hit the dashboard. "Who's shooting?"

"The guys in the SUV."

"Who're the guys in the SUV?" My voice was not my own. I sounded like SpongeBob SquarePants. "Why are they shooting?"

"I don't know," she said through her teeth, as if my questions were annoying her. "Just stay down."

Really? *Really?* Was it too much to ask her to tell me why I was being shot at? And did she really think she *needed* to tell me to stay down? What am I, stupid? I may have spent some time in and out of the hospital but never for a gunshot wound, and I didn't feel like starting today.

Kaia's eyes narrowed as she glanced at the rearview mirror. "Damn it. That's not even the same SUV I saw at the house. I guess Picklebreath was right."

What, the hell, was she talking about? For the first time it occurred to me that maybe Kaia wasn't entirely there. Did she have a concussion? Considering the egg on her forehead, it was definitely possible, which meant she probably shouldn't have been behind the wheel of a car, let alone driving it at ninety-five miles an hour.

I imagined reaching over and taking the wheel, easing the truck to the side of the road, dialing 911. Maybe we'd spend the weekend on her couch while she recovered. I'd bring her french fries and coffee ice cream—her favorite disgusting snack—and we'd curl up together to watch a *Walking Dead* marathon. Perfection.

Another shot rang out. And I remembered the blood at the house. The man on the ground. The knife near his hand. And the gun. Kaia and the gun.

My pulse pounded in my ears. I watched the sky rush past the window as Kaia swerved the car in and out of traffic, inching the speedometer up and up and up. There was another blast and I bit down on my tongue to keep from screaming.

Suddenly, Kaia slammed on the brakes, downshifted, and spun the car in a complete 180. The greasy pizza I'd scarfed earlier shifted inside my gut. It reminded me that we were supposed to be meeting Brian and Grace for a double date at the movie theater downtown. I'd so been looking forward to the free popcorn my friend Hunter, who worked there, would slip us. Brian and I had this whole plan to get our girlfriends to bond so we could hang out more. But I guess that was no longer happening.

Outside the car there was a deafening screech and a prolonged crunch of metal. The scent of burned rubber filled my nostrils, which didn't help the I'm-going-to-toss-my-lunch feeling rising up inside my throat.

"What're you—"

"Oliver, I love you, but not now."

She hunched over the wheel, eyes fierce, jaw clenched, and gunned the engine again. Tires screamed. Kaia slammed the wheel to the right, and the hood of the truck dipped so drastically

I was sure we were diving off a cliff, but in the next second we bumped up again on flat road.

One of the first things that had attracted me to Kaia was that she didn't give a crap about the superficial stuff the other girls at school were obsessed with. She was a tomboy. She could skateboard. She liked to run and bike and could do as many push-ups as me. She never wore makeup and laughed at gross jokes and could eat like a truck driver. And now I could chalk up another talent to the growing list. The girl could drive like a mofo.

I sat up a little, dying to see where we were, and tried to catch my breath. She took an off-ramp onto a smaller highway with fewer cars. I looked behind us. Smoke billowed toward the sky in the distance, but there was no SUV in sight. Thick trees lined the road, their leaves fluttering in the breeze. Kaia let out a breath and leaned back in the driver's seat. She reached up to touch the gold locket she always wore around her neck—the one with the tiny pictures of her and her dad inside. A raindrop hit the windshield, and I flinched.

My throat was so jammed with questions I couldn't seem to make my voice box work.

"Oliver. You're staring," Kaia said, with the wry smile I was so used to seeing. On, you know, a normal day.

"I...I don't...are you going to tell me what's going on?"

She was silent. Raindrops battered the windshield in sporadic waves, as if we were driving though bursts of gunfire and not under steel gray storm clouds.

"Yes," she said finally. "When we get there."

"Get where?"

She looked over at me, and her eyes softened. "I could tell you, but then I'd have to kill you."

chapter 3

KAIA

I DON'T THINK I BREATHED AGAIN UNTIL I SAW THE SMALL, WOOD-shingled garage appear around the bend in the dirt road two hours later. A moment after that, I exhaled.

The house was still there. After everything that had happened this afternoon, I wouldn't have been surprised to find out I'd dreamed this place. Or that I'd forgotten how to get here. Thankfully, Oliver had stopped talking, except to mutter the occasional "Where the hell *are* we?" or "Robin is going to murder me." He'd already texted Brian to tell him we weren't going to make it to the movies—it was so cute he thought that still mattered—and now, he sat forward in his seat to squint at the uneven green siding. I brought the truck to a stop, picked up my phone, and tried Bess again.

Voice mail.

I tried Henry.

Voice mail.

Gritting my teeth, I ended the call.

"Get out," I said.

I'd gone Alpha Girl. Maybe it was because I was going to have to tell him the truth, and this was my psyche's way of putting up defensive walls for the inevitable screaming match and breakup. Oliver and I had never fought before, not once in the year we'd been together, and the idea of starting now made my heart hurt. At least my bossiness seemed to be working on him. Without question, he got out of the truck.

I grabbed the German's bag from the truck bed, then tromped over to the garage and yanked the rickety old door. It let out an ear-piercing shriek as it yawned open, metal scraping against metal. The car was still there. A 2010 Honda Accord, black. There were thousands of these on the road, so it was perfect for blending in. I glanced at the stack of license plates in the corner. Twenty different states represented. I could deal with that later.

"Kaia?" Oliver ventured, hovering off to my right.

There was a catch in my chest.

"Inside," I said.

He made an impatient noise as I walked past him. My face was on fire, and my eyes hurt from not meeting his. I retrieved the key from behind the shingle fourth from the bottom, under the second window. The sight of the Thor key chain almost killed me. *Dad.* I opened the door.

Inside, the house was cool and smelled of wood and dust. I dropped the bag and flicked the light switch. The overhead fixtures buzzed and illuminated the modest living room/kitchen combo in soft, yellow light. Oliver walked in behind me, his heavy steps making the floorboards groan.

"Close the door," I said.

He did, with a bang. "That's the last order I'm going to take until you tell me where the hell we are and what's going on."

"We're in Fredericksburg, South Carolina, about half an hour's drive from the Tennessee border." I dropped my backpack on the kitchen counter and opened the first cabinet. Canned food. Soup. Vegetables. Peanut butter. Boxes of crackers. I pulled one down. It didn't expire for another year. I shoved the crackers and peanut butter into my bag.

"No, I mean, I know where we are. I can read road signs." Oliver sounded exasperated. "But what *is* this place? Some kind of hunting cabin?"

It was a fair assumption, considering we were in the middle of the forest and there was a gun case on the living room wall, locked, though the key was also on the key chain in my pocket. Inside the second cabinet, I found a silver box that contained passports. Five for my mother, three for my father, one for me. Mine included a picture of me at twelve years old and proclaimed my name to be Jessica Martinez. I took it and pushed it into my back pocket.

"This is a safe house," I said. "My parents set it up in case something like this ever happened."

A wide drawer contained a set of leather-sheathed hunting knives. I picked one at random. I really hated knives—didn't love the idea of having to be close enough to my attacker to use one—but my mother would have told me to take one just in case, so I did. Oliver eyed me warily, and I felt a thump of self-consciousness. I'd never been a girly girl, a dress-wearer, a high-heeled lip-glossy chick like 80 percent of the girls at my school. And I knew that Oliver liked that about me. But now he was seeing a side of me I'd managed to keep hidden all this time—my commando mode. I didn't even want to know what he was thinking as I shoved the knife into my waistband.

"Wait. A safe house? Like in spy movies?" He laughed nervously. "Kaia, you said your parents were insurance adjusters."

I shot him an apologetic look over my shoulder. His face fell. In the next cabinet, I found the money. Stacks of it.

"What the…?" Oliver walked to my side. "Where did all that cash come from? Is that yours?"

"Yep. Technically."

I didn't count it. I quickly took the stacks down one by one and pushed them into the bottom of my backpack. Those were my practical parents for you. Always prepared. Thank you, Mom and Dad.

Oliver grabbed my wrist, not so hard it hurt, but firmly. He meant business. Unfortunately, his touch made me want to huddle against him. For the last year, the warm curl of Oliver's arms was the only place I'd felt safe. You'd think that after losing both my parents on one day, I'd be afraid to love anyone else. That was how a lot of people react to loss, right? By shutting down, constructing walls around their heart. But not me. I'd gone the opposite route. When my parents disappeared they'd left me with all this love to give and no one to share it with. The moment I'd met Oliver, the moment I'd looked into his eyes and realized that he saw me, that he understood me, I was a goner. I'd never had a real friend before, let alone a boyfriend. All my life it had been no one but me and my parents, with occasional guest appearances from Uncle Marco. Not a soul had ever spared me a glance, let alone a look like that.

And he was so kind to me. So patient with my insomnia and my exhaustion. So willing to hang out at my house watching movies when his popular friends were throwing their popular-people-parties that were probably way more fun. He gave me everything, so I gave him everything right back. Including my heart. And now, I was going to have to leave him behind.

"Kaia, I swear if you don't tell me what's going on, my head is going to explode."

I swallowed my fear. There was no getting around this. He deserved to know why I'd landed him in harm's way and basically kidnapped him and dragged him out to the middle of nowhere. He deserved to know why I was going to have to break up with him.

"Okay, but I need you to listen, because I'm only going to say this once."

Oliver stepped back. He crossed his arms over his chest, which made his muscles bulge, which was really unfair because he knew how much I loved his arms. But I also loved his back. His legs. His hair. His eyes. All of him.

Shit. This was going to hurt.

"My parents were hired assassins," I told him, keeping my voice steady. His jaw dropped, but before he could interrupt, I soldiered on. "They were both in the military after college, but then they were recruited by the CIA. They were in a black ops unit that carried out assassinations and kidnappings on behalf of the US government."

Oliver backed up until his butt hit the rear of the couch, and he leaned into it. "So, not insurance adjusters, then?"

"Nope." I crossed the living room to the closet. "That was a lie. Sorry."

"Okay, so that guy back there was…?"

I grabbed a sleeping bag out of the closet, along with a duffel bag full of never-worn women's clothes. Clothes meant for my mother to wear someday. Utilitarian stuff like cargo pants, long-sleeved T-shirts, and a Windbreaker. There was a pair of black sneakers with a hot-pink stripe at the bottom of the bag. That hot-pink stripe shattered my heart.

Mom. She always did love her pink.

"Are you okay?" Oliver asked.

"Check his bag."

"What?"

"The guy's bag. I took it with me." I walked past Oliver and crouched next to the well-worn leather weekender. Inside were several neatly folded soft shirts, a pair of running shoes, and a Dopp kit. All of it smelled like stale cigarette smoke. In the side zipper pocket I hit pay dirt. His passport and a tablet. I chucked the passport at Oliver, who caught it, and then powered up the tablet.

"Password protected," I muttered, and tossed it aside. I was no hacker, and I definitely didn't have time to figure out some random dude's password.

"Dieter Morschauser," Oliver read. He turned the photo toward me. Shockingly, the man was smiling.

"Where's he from?" I asked, rising to my feet.

"Hamburg, Germany."

So this *was* about the Hamburg job. But how had this guy known where to find me? And why did he think my mom was alive? I swallowed hard, trying to squelch a flicker of hope. *Was* my mom alive?

"Why was some guy from Hamburg, Germany…" Oliver took a couple steps toward me and reached for my face. His thumb grazed the spot where the knifepoint had been a few hours ago. A pang of pain. "He hurt you."

I went against every instinct and turned away from him. "I'm fine. And he was there because he was sent to kill me." *After he got information out of me.*

"What? Why?"

"When I was little, my parents quit the CIA and went to work for themselves. They became hired guns. High-end hit men." I went back to the closet and tossed the duffel and sleeping bag on the floor at his feet, then met his gaze for the first time in hours. He looked shocked but not scared or disgusted. That was something, at least. "I traveled the world with them while they carried out their missions. Unless they decided a job was too dangerous. Then they'd leave me behind with my uncle, Marco."

Lie. My parents took me with them everywhere. They were convinced that I was never safer than when I was by their sides. And they never would have left me with Marco. If they had, they would have come home to find me eating cheese curls and slugging soda in front of a pirated WWE pay-per-view boxing match while surrounded by pot-smoking gambling addicts with bad teeth. At least when I was with them, they could homeschool me, monitor my Internet searches, make sure I went to bed on time and had healthy food in my belly. Marco would never have known what to do with me. Unless he tried to get me to work a con.

But I needed to tell that little white lie to support my next, bigger one. It was a lie I had to tell because I didn't want to talk about what had really happened. I would never, ever want to talk about it.

"My parents were on a mission last year when they disappeared," I told him, as if I hadn't been there. As if I'd seen nothing. "Both of them."

Oliver blinked. "Wow. That's...that's—"

"Insane? I know. Believe me, I know. But it was our life. I didn't know anything different until..."

You, I wanted to say. *You were the first normal part of my life. Ever.*

But I was afraid to say it, because I knew my voice would crack, and I couldn't be weak. Not now.

"Anyway, that's why that guy came after me. To get revenge for one of their jobs."

"Kaia, I'm so sorry," Oliver said, still holding the German's passport. "About your parents, I mean."

"You already knew they were dead," I said, more harshly than I intended.

I'd told him they'd died in a car crash. That I was an orphan. That this was why I was living with my grandparents. But Henry and Bess were not my grandparents. I'd met them for the very first time when I'd shown up on their doorstep last year. They were old colleagues of my parents and had taken me in out of loyalty to them. Henry and Bess had cared for me, fed me, clothed me, even helped me with my homework.

All that blood... Could they have possibly survived?

"Yeah, I know." Oliver took my hand. "But this...this is different. Not knowing, having to wonder if they're out there. If they're ever coming back."

My chest constricted. Oliver knew how it felt. His mother had passed away when he was only eight years old, and then his rat-bastard father had abandoned him. Left him at the mercy of the system with nothing but an old soccer ball and a picture of is mom. And even though the man sounded like a worthless piece of crap, he was still Oliver's father. He was still out there, living a life. Sending Oliver cards on his birthday but never with a return address, always with a postmark from a different part of the country. But wherever he was, there existed the possibility he might straighten up, realize what he'd lost, and come back for his son.

My situation was not the same.

"They're not," I told him firmly, slipping my hand from his. "My parents are dead, Oliver."

I grabbed the duffel, the sleeping bag, and my backpack and left them by the door.

"But how do you know—"

"I know. Because if they were alive, they would have come for me," I told him, shoving down that flicker of hope. It had taken forever for me to come to terms with the fact that I was never going to see them again. I couldn't go back to wishful thinking. "If they were alive, they'd be here right now."

A look came over Oliver's face, like I'd offended him somehow. Maybe I had. Maybe I was implying that my parents were better than his dad. That they would never, ever leave me by choice, when that was exactly what his father had done. But it was the truth. The Thompson family stuck together, no matter what. It was the only truth I'd ever known. If I didn't believe it, my parents were not only gone, but I had never known them in the first place. If I didn't believe it, I had nothing.

Oliver tossed the German's passport at the leather bag. It slid across the top and hit the floor. A scrap of paper fluttered out onto the floor, attached to a paper clip.

"What's that?" I asked.

Oliver plucked it up. "It's a bunch of numbers."

He held out the scrap to me. It was numbers—but they weren't random. "They're coordinates. Eight sets." And the first four had been scratched through.

"Coordinates for what?" Oliver asked.

"I don't know. I'll look them up later." I shoved the scrap in my pocket and yanked open the front door, effectively cutting off whatever he was going to say next.

"Come on," I said. "We have to move."

chapter 4

OLIVER

THE SUN WAS GOING DOWN AS I FOLLOWED KAIA THROUGH THE woods. My phone kept dinging, but I refused to look at it. I'd already texted Brian to tell him Kaia's grandmother wasn't feeling well, so we had to skip the movie to help out. Which he probably took to mean that Kaia hated his girlfriend, Grace, and she was making up excuses, but whatever. I had bigger things to think about than hurting Grace's feelings. If it wasn't Brian texting me, it was Robin. And I *really* didn't want to read her texts. She was expecting me home half an hour ago.

About fifty paces into the trees, Kaia took out the huge knife she'd found back at the safe house—was I really throwing around words like "safe house"?—and slashed the trunk of a tree.

"What'd that tree ever do to you?" I said, trying to lighten things up a little.

"I'm marking our trail."

Okay. So Kaia was not in the mood for jokes. She kept moving, cutting trees here and there, vaulting over fallen limbs, and scrambling over rocks like someone out of *The Hunger*

Games. I shook my head, trying to process what was happening. My girlfriend was the daughter of trained assassins. She knew how to use a gun and wield a knife. She was in possession of more money than I'd ever seen in my life.

The second I saw those stacks of cash I'd started to sweat. Because the things I could do with money like that... I could buy a car. I could finally tell my foster father, Jack, to back the fuck off. I could run away and take Kaia with me—the daydream to end all daydreams come true.

And Kaia had acted as if it was a given that the cash would be there. She'd shoved the bills into her bag like it was nothing. Was Kaia's family rich? They must have been to leave thousands of dollars hidden at unused safe houses. But she never acted rich. Kaia owned, like, one pair of boots and two pairs of sneakers. And yes, a dozen skateboards and an iPad, but practically everyone I knew had an iPad. I'd only used the ones bolted to the table in the school library.

"What're you gonna do with all that cash?" I asked Kaia as she paused to catch her breath.

"Use it to survive," she said. "Until I find out what happened to Henry and Bess and whether it's safe to go back."

"Henry and Bess?"

"They weren't really my grandparents," Kaia said.

I pictured Kaia's grandfather and grandmother as I'd known them. Him large, straight-backed, and intimidating; her sweet, soft, and wrinkled. I'd once told Kaia that she had her grandmother's eyes. Joke was on me I guess. "Wait—weren't?"

"That much blood..." she trailed off. "It's not promising. And they're not answering their phones."

My heart twisted as she shoved aside a branch. Here I was imagining my getaway from Robin and Jack, who had at least put a roof over my head for the last nine years—ever since my dad bailed and I was placed with them by social services—and Kaia had no idea if the people she'd been staying with were even alive, if she'd ever have a home to go back to. Suddenly I felt like a selfish jackass.

But then, out of nowhere, this heady feeling came over me and my heart started to pound. My favorite daydream wasn't just a daydream anymore—it was happening. I'd always thought the hard part would be the leaving, but Kaia and I were already gone. If she had no family, and I had no family and if she had a bag full of cash, then we could start over together. I could totally get a job to support us. I could get my mechanic's license, easy. We could be together forever. We could be free.

It would be hard, leaving Trevor behind. We might not have been technically related—him being the son of my foster parents—but he was the closest thing to family I had outside of Kaia. Still, what was the alternative? Going back to Robin and Jack's and kidnapping him? Even I wasn't optimistic enough to think that Kaia and I could take care of a ten-year-old with Asperger's without help. Without his therapists. And there was also the whole fact that it would be *kidnapping*. No matter what I said to him to make him feel safe inside his own home on a daily basis, I couldn't be there for him forever, even though I wanted to.

"You coming?" Kaia asked over her shoulder.

I cleared my throat. "Yeah."

About fifteen minutes into our hike, the sky went from pink to purple. By this time, Robin was definitely wondering where I was. Not that I cared. When had she ever shown that she cared about me? When she stood aside while her estranged husband kicked me in the face? When she sent me to school without lunch because she'd spent all her extra cash bailing him out of jail—again? Let her wonder. I mean, honestly? I might never see her again.

But what if Jack showed up in one of his moods and there was no one there to shield Trevor?

My lungs constricted, and I curled my fingers into fists until the stab of panic eased. There was nothing I could do for Trevor right now. I was a good couple hours away. If Jack came by to see his son tonight, Robin was going to have to step up and protect him. For once.

I ignored the little voice in my head telling me that she wouldn't, that she never had and never would. She'd long ago delegated the job of protector and professional punching bag to me. It was the one thing I'd never told Kaia about my life. My one big secret.

Secrets.

"Kaia…was anything you told me about yourself true?"

She paused and looked at me. For the first time in hours, she seemed like herself. Or at least the version of her I knew. Her eyes were soft and in the waning light, her freckles stood out across her nose. But she still had the lump on her forehead, and the red scratches on her face had darkened to black.

"I really do love french fries."

I smirked. "And ice cream."

"So very much," she said with a longing sigh.

For a split second, I thought about kissing her. I wanted to tell her that I understood why she'd lied to me and that everything was going to be all right. But there was so much that I *didn't* understand—like what had happened back at her house. Why, if her parents were dead, would anyone be coming after her? It wasn't like she'd ever done anything to hurt anyone. And how the heck could I know if we were going to be okay? But there was one thing that needed to be said.

"I love you, you know. I don't care what your parents did." I took her hand—the one not holding a weapon—and pulled her to me. My fingers ran over her hair, smoothing it down the back of her head, then cupping it against her neck. There was nothing I loved to do more than touch her hair. "I love you, Kaia."

Her smiled waned. "I know."

That was not the reaction I'd been expecting. She started walking again, and it took me a second to catch up. Panic started to tickle my gut, but I refused to acknowledge it. She was obviously stressed. That look had meant nothing.

"So the people in the SUV, back at your house?" I asked. "Were they with this Dieter guy?"

Kaia shrugged one shoulder and impaled another tree. "Maybe. Maybe not."

I climbed over a large, rotted tree trunk, trying to keep up with her. "Well, why were they shooting at us?"

Kaia paused and glanced around. "I assume because they want me dead, whoever they are. Dieter said there would be others coming."

"Others?" I tripped over a rock and would have fallen into her, taking her down with me, but at the last second I grabbed a thick tree branch and saved us both.

"Are you okay?" Kaia asked.

"Fine," I said, embarrassed, dusting bits of tree bark off my palm. "I'm fine."

"Good," she said. "'Cause we're here."

Suddenly I could hear the whoosh of traffic, see the flash of headlights in the near distance.

Before I could ask where we were, Kaia was already on the move. We emerged into the rear parking lot of a small gas station market. The Dumpster near the back door was overflowing with garbage, and the air reeked of rotting food and fresh exhaust. Kaia walked toward the front of the place, the parking lot lights elongating her shadow. Around the corner, a couple of guys smoked cigarettes and discussed the upcoming Panthers game. They stopped when they saw Kaia and blatantly checked her out. She didn't notice. I tried to ignore them.

"Kaia, what do you mean, 'others'?" I whispered again. "Other Germans? Other…bad guys?" It sounded idiotic the moment the words left my lips. "Are we talking a couple of random people here, or an army?"

"I don't really know," she said calmly. "I don't even know if he was telling the truth."

We went inside the shop. Kaia panned the store, like she always did whenever we entered a room. Now I knew why. She was scanning the place for enemies. Probably a habit she developed on all her "missions." Seemingly deciding the coast was clear, she ducked down a short aisle filled with processed baked goods. She picked up a cylinder of powdered donuts and handed them to me. My favorite.

"You have your cell phone, right?" she asked.

"Yeah, why?"

I pulled it from my pocket. My prized possession. I'd worked a lot of hours at minimum wage selling replacement windshield wiper blades and car batteries at the downtown auto parts store and body shop to buy it and pay for its monthly plan. I still got a happy feeling whenever I held the thing. Not that I'd ever tell anyone that. The job was totally worth it, and not just for the phone. Hank Fusco, the guy who owned the place, was helping me salvage parts to restore a crappy old Chevy to working order. And when we were finished, he was going to let me keep it.

We were months from being done. But at least it gave me something to look forward to. I spent hours, days, fantasizing about Kaia and me driving off into the sunset in that car.

Kaia went to the refrigerated aisle at the back of the store and took out a single-serve bottle of chocolate milk. Also my favorite.

"Call Brian. Or Hunter. Tell them to come pick you up."

She tried to hand me the milk, but I took a step back. "Wait. Pick me up? You're not coming?"

"Oliver, I told you five seconds ago, I can't go back there right now."

"Kaia, what are *you* gonna do? Stay here?"

"Yes." Her gaze darted to the door as it swung open. The smokers were coming inside. They made their way to the far end of the store, where the slushie machine lived. "I'm going to hang out at the safe house for a few days and figure out my next move. Maybe I'll try to track down my uncle Marco and see if he knows what's going on. My parents always told me that if anything ever happened to them I wasn't supposed to contact anyone from my old life, but this seems like a worst-case scenario situation."

"Okay then," I said, my pulse racing. "I'll stay with you."

Kaia snorted. "Oliver, you can't. You have a life. And I may have to travel. I may have to go to Marco, wherever the hell he is."

"So I'll go with you," I said, though my throat was dry. The daydream was slowly fading in my mind. How could she not see the opportunity this nightmare had given us—to be alone together? To get the hell out? Besides, Kaia had never mentioned an uncle before today. Who was he? What was his deal? Was he in "the family business" too?

She crossed her arms over her chest, still holding the milk bottle in one hand. "What if those guys find me again? I don't know if I can fight them off and keep you safe."

"Keep me safe?" I balked. "Are you *trying* to crush my manhood?"

"Oliver, come on," she said, her voice condescending. "You know what I mean. I want you to go home because I care about you. It's the only way I'll know you're okay."

The irony of that statement was so thick I could have choked on it. I was anything but okay when I was at home. At home, I was Jack's recreational kickboxing dummy. He took out all the frustrations of his sorry-ass life on me. At home, I was always one left hook away from the ICU. But Kaia didn't know that. After my last trip to the hospital with a festering black eye, Jack got really good at keeping the bruises centralized in places I could hide them, and I got really good at hiding them. Across the room, the Panthers fans cackled.

"Oliver," Kaia said again, mistaking my silence as stubbornness. "I'm sorry, but if you come with me, you'll be a liability."

I was about to tell her that she'd hit below the belt, when the door opened and her face went white. I hadn't seen her look that pale since the morning we'd met. That morning had changed everything. I could still remember the scent of cafeteria french toast that hung in the air, how some of her thick hair was still wet from her shower even hours into the school day, the way her T-shirt had been tucked half-in, half-out of her jeans. And she thought I was going to leave her?

I turned to see two men. One was tall, sleek, and handsome in a ballroom dancer sort of way. Except he had this nasty, jagged, purple scar from the tip of his ear, down his cheek to his chin. The other man was broad-shouldered and tough-looking, the kind of guy who would rather punch you in the face than argue his point. He had a wide, flat nose, a healthy black beard, and fleshy cheeks that seemed to hang down over his collar. They both wore sleek leather jackets, pressed shirts, and too much jewelry. They couldn't have been more out of place in the forests of northern South Carolina if they'd been sporting pink wigs.

Kaia hit the floor so fast that for a second I thought she fainted. Then she grabbed my hand and dragged me down with her. My kneecap smacked the tile floor and I bit my lip to keep from cursing.

"Oh my God," she said under her breath. "Ohmygod-ohmygodohmygod."

"What? What is it?" I hissed.

"We have to get out of here." She spoke through her teeth. "We have to go. *Now*."

There was an unmarked door behind her, maybe leading to a stock room or to the back lot where we'd come out of the woods. I tilted my head toward the door and she nodded. We crawled over on hands and knees, ignoring the sheen of filth on the floor. As I pushed the door open with one hand, the man with the scar spoke. He had a thick Mexican accent.

"She's about this tall…got dark hair, blue eyes…freckles… Have you seen her?"

Outside we scrambled to our feet, just as the thug came around the corner. He must have walked out the front door half a second after he'd walked in. He startled at the sight of us, then flicked a smile. One of his front top teeth was missing.

"That was almost too easy." He pointed a thick finger at Kaia. "You. You're comin' with me."

What happened next was a blur. The guy lunged for Kaia. I spun and launched my foot at his face. A perfect spin kick. My heavy work boot collided with his jaw and there was a satis-fying *crack.* Kaia screamed. The guy hit the asphalt, knocking his cheek against a pile of cement bricks near the door. Blood oozed everywhere.

"Sonofabitch!" he shouted.

Still on the ground, he grabbed one of the bricks and took a swing at me, catching my leg. The cut stung, but it was only a graze. I hit him with a front-kick under the chin and his head snapped back.

"Oliver!" Kaia shouted.

The thug collided with the ground, and this time his eyes fluttered closed. He was out cold.

Huh. That, I'd never done before. At least not for real. I was so hopped up on adrenaline I almost laughed.

"Not much of a fighter, are ya, big guy?" I commented, spitting on the ground. I'd seen dozens of badasses do this in movies, but it wasn't as satisfying as I thought it would be. I wiped my bottom lip with the back of my hand.

"What the hell was that?" Kaia asked, shaking as she came up beside me. "He has a gun!"

Startled, I looked down at my opponent. His jacket had fallen open and sure enough, he wore a leather holster with a pretty big weapon strapped into it.

"Well, he didn't get to use it," I said, my voice high and reedy.

"Oliver, where the hell did you learn to do that?"

Kaia shoved my shoulder with one hand—the hand that still held the bottle of chocolate milk. I still held the sleeve of donuts. We'd shoplifted and I didn't even care. My chest heaved as I stared at Kaia.

"Still think I'm a liability?"

chapter 5

KAIA

SOMETHING CRASHED INSIDE THE BUILDING. OLIVER AND I LOCKED eyes. There was no time for more questions. I grabbed his hand and we ran, taking off into the trees. All I could think about was putting as much distance as possible between us and that man. Scarface. I'd seen him in my nightmares countless times over the past year, leering at me, threatening my mother. His was a face I would never forget.

But what the hell was he doing here? Why was he looking for me? Was he who the German had meant by *others*? Did Picklebreath and Scarface somehow know each other?

Impossible. They were from opposite ends of the world. But it couldn't be a coincidence that they'd both found me on the same freaking day. And what did they have in common? My parents. More specifically, my mom.

At the very base of my skull, I felt an odd sort of tingling. It couldn't be…could it?

Maybe I *should* spend a little time trying to hack into the

German's tablet. At the very least, I had to figure out what those coordinates meant.

Under the thick canopy of branches and leaves, it was almost entirely dark, but I was still able to see the jagged white slashes I'd made in the trees along our route. My terror made me fast, and Oliver—ever the athlete—kept pace with me. It took less than ten minutes to get back to the cabin. We emerged onto the dirt driveway and I bent over, heaving for air, my hands and a bottle of well-shaken chocolate milk, braced above my knees.

One breath. Two. Three. That was all I'd give myself. I got behind the wheel of the Honda, praying the keys would be in the ignition. I didn't have time to conduct a search. Thankfully, the keys were there. Another Thor key chain. Dad was nothing if not a die-hard fan. Of the comics that is, not the movies. After a few ominous clicks, the car started. I hit reverse and slammed on the gas, kicking up dirt. Oliver watched from a safe distance as I left the car door open, jogged into the house and grabbed the bags I'd left on the floor inside.

"What're you doing? I thought you were staying here," Oliver said.

"Not anymore," I replied, tossing everything into the backseat and slamming the door.

Oliver blinked. I could tell he had a zillion questions as he looked over his shoulder toward the woods, but instead of grilling me, he asked, "What can I do?"

I hesitated before answering. "Back inside. I need more food."

We raced into the cabin together. Oliver went to the cabinets and yanked out cans of soup and fruit. I found the camp stove under the sink—kerosene, a lighter, a can opener. With the items cradled in one arm, I paused on my way through the living room. Then I went to the closet and grabbed the second duffel—the one with my dad's clothes inside—and another sleeping bag. Oliver and I walked outside together and threw everything into the backseat. Then I went to the truck and grabbed my skateboard. It was my oldest—and my favorite. It was a basic black board with lime-green wheels and a peace sign I'd painted on with a Wite-Out marker when I was twelve. At the time, I'd thought it would be a sign of rebellion to my parents. I'd named her Sophia because we'd been in France when Dad had brought her home for me. Well, to the hole-in-the-wall hotel we'd been staying in.

The car was still running. I pulled Henry's truck into the garage and locked it. Back inside the cabin, my hand shook as I unlocked the gun cabinet. I left the shot guns and selected a sleek, little Beretta Pico—the exact gun I'd learned to shoot at the range back in Houston—and enough bullets to stop the Incredible Hulk. (The Hulk was never my dad's favorite. He preferred heroes who had some level of control over their emotional shit.)

Back outside, I locked the door behind me and returned the keys to their hiding spot.

Oliver followed me to the car. He walked around to the

passenger door. My hand found the handle on the driver's side. We looked at each other over the roof.

I had clothes for him. A sleeping bag. But I could still change my mind. I could still send him home where he'd be safe. I had no idea where I was going, who else might be following me, what Scarface would do to me if he caught up. I might have to sleep in shelters or alleyways. I might have to pay off bookies or dealers to find Marco. I might have to fight for my life.

Could I do all of that with Oliver? Could I do it without him?

Without him.

The words reverberated inside my chest, tying my heartstrings into knots.

"Get in."

Oliver smiled, and did as he was told.

I didn't speak again until we'd navigated the twisty dirt driveway in the dark—no headlights so as not to attract attention—and made it out to the main highway. My palms were so slick they slipped on the wheel.

"Where did you learn to do that spin kick move?" I asked again, looking at Oliver from the corner of my eye.

Oliver smirked. The air whooshing through the cracked windows had turned cold, and he'd found a black, zip-front jacket in the bag. Classic Oliver. He preferred fresh air to a closed car, always—even if it meant bundling up. He looked gorgeous with the collar zipped all the way up to his chin. Older. More rugged.

"I could tell you," he said, "but then I'd have to kill you."

I smirked back, even as my stomach curled in on itself. I trusted Oliver more than anyone else in my life. I didn't like to think he kept secrets from me, though I realized how big of a hypocrite that made me. "Touché."

"So who was that guy back there?" Oliver asked, pushing back his seat. He ripped open the sleeve of donuts and offered me one. I shook my head. "Just the sight of him scared the hell out of you."

My fingers regripped the wheel. I still couldn't believe I'd actually seen Scarface. He'd been haunting my sleep for so long that seeing him while wide-awake seemed impossible. And yet...

"The last hit my parents were supposed to carry out...the trip where they disappeared," I started, then trailed off. "It had something to do with a shady Mexican politician." In fact, my dad had been paid to take out said shady Mexican politician. But that had never happened. "I'm pretty sure Scarface was one of the people involved."

Another lie. I was totally sure it was him. Scarface had been there the day my parents disappeared. He might even know where they were, what had happened to them. But he wasn't the type of person you walked up to and struck up a conversation with. He was the type of person from whom you ran.

"Scarface?" Oliver asked. "Is that his actual name?"

I shook my head. "I don't know what his name is. I made it up."

"Appropriate," Oliver joked.

"I thought so," I said, struggling to keep my voice even. "And up until now, I was pretty sure he killed my mom."

"Holy…" Oliver turned to look at me. Powdered sugar rimmed his lips. "Up until now? What's changed?"

"I don't know. I keep thinking…"

I was still having a hard time wrapping my brain around the possibility that she was alive. Saying it out loud would make that hope real. It had been a really long time since I'd allowed myself to hope.

"Why would that guy be looking for me?" I asked finally. "What reason could he possibly have for coming after me?" I took a breath and blew it out. "He either wants to kill me to send a message or kidnap me to use me as bait."

"There's a sentence I never thought I'd hear you say." He smiled, his cheek full of donut.

I tried to sound normal despite the tightness in my chest. "You're taking all of this pretty well."

Maybe too well. I couldn't put my finger on what, but something was off. Or maybe it was the fact that my entire world had been thrown askew. Again.

"What do you mean?" he asked.

"I mean, I just told you my parents killed people for a living and that there are criminals after me who probably want me dead, and you're sitting there chowing on donuts."

Oliver looked down at the last remaining sugar-covered O. "I eat when I'm stressed."

"No you don't."

A pair of headlights appeared in the rearview. I eased into the slow lane to see if the car would pass. It did.

"Yes. I do. Do you not recall a certain extra-large buffalo chicken pizza I ate *by myself* studying for Crackpot's history final last year?"

"Oh, yeah. That." I wrinkled my nose. Crackpot was the nickname for Mr. Kirkpatrick, our school's endlessly cranky US One teacher, known for writing essay questions not even a textbook author could answer. "I thought you were just hungry."

"I was, but I also chased it with a box of Twinkies."

I laughed. "How the hell did you keep all that down?"

"Believe me. It took some effort." Oliver smiled. "So...you think that guy back there wants to use you as bait. For what?"

I pressed my tongue against the top of my dry mouth. I couldn't believe what I was about to say, but it was the only logical explanation. Why else would Scarface be hanging out in the backwoods of South Carolina? Why would he describe me to random gas station attendants? I reached up to touch my hair. It might be time for a new cut. And a serious color change.

"I think that the fact that he's here means one or both of my parents is still alive."

"Wow," Oliver said. "You think?"

"Well...who else could he draw out by coming after me?"

After more than a year of searching the Internet for mentions of my parents, forcing Bess to call old contacts in the army, scouring my brain for clues and finally accepting there was no way they would have left me for this long if they *were* alive, there was no way they would have missed a birthday and a Christmas…there was hope.

"Wow," Oliver said again, swallowing.

My parents could still be alive. I might be able to find them. I might be able to see them again. To hear their voices. To hold them. My head felt light. I reached up to rub my mother's locket between my thumb and forefinger, and for the first time in a long time, I allowed myself to truly remember them.

I saw my father on the beach in Saint Lucia, grabbing my mother from behind and twirling her off her feet, the two of them laughing as the sun glinted off their tanned skin. I saw my dad sitting by my bed in the middle of the night, trying not to nod off in case I needed anything while I was fighting croup, and my mother bringing him a cup of steaming coffee accompanied by a kiss on the forehead. I saw my mother baking brownies for my birthday, my dad scooping batter from the bowl with his finger, then—when she got annoyed—offering it to her instead of eating it himself. A food fight had ensued, only ending when we were all covered in chocolate. We'd all showered, then gone out for ice cream instead.

My parents. Alive. It was possible. But if they were alive, where the hell were they? Where had they been all this time? Why had they left me?

"Are you okay?" Oliver asked. He placed his hand on my leg, the warmth of his palm permeating my jeans and tingling my skin.

"I'm fine," I assured him.

But I wasn't. My thoughts were racing in a thousand different directions, every zigzagging path ending in an unanswerable question.

As he pulled his hand back again, digging in the plastic wrap for the last donut, I eyed him surreptitiously. He really did look older with his slightly sweaty hair pushed back from his face, that black jacket hugging his shoulders. How much did I really know about Oliver Lange? Why did Mr. Popularity with the two varsity letters and straight-A average need to know self-defense? If he was taking martial arts classes, why didn't I know about it?

My mother had once told me you couldn't trust people who came into your life at the exact moment you needed them.

Real life doesn't work that way, Kiki, she'd said. *If it seems too good to be true, it probably is.*

I'd never thought about it before. Why would I? Oliver was Oliver. Sweet, soccer-playing foster kid Oliver. But now I couldn't seem to stop thinking about it.

My mom had basically paid the one friend I'd ever had to hang out with me. We'd been on a three-month recon mission in Italy when I was eleven, and my mother had suddenly decided I needed socialization, so she'd gotten me a nanny— Francesca—who'd come with her own daughter, Nita. Nita and I had done everything together. Had sleepovers, raced skateboards, created stupid skits and forced our parents to watch them. I'd thought we'd be best friends forever. But when the job was over, so was the friendship. I'd emailed Nita about four dozen times after we left Italy, but she'd never emailed me back. Not once.

Could Oliver possibly be more of the same? Was he another one of my parent's contingency plans like Henry and Bess? A prearranged friend for their freak loner daughter in case they left me an orphan?

Honestly? I wouldn't have put it past my mom. Her level of planning was absurd.

It occurred to me that I could ask Oliver. *Did you know my parents? Are you actually a twentysomething manny posing as a seventeen-year-old?* But it sounded absurd when I put it into words. And what if he'd been paid by someone else to befriend me? Another enemy who wanted to use me to get to my parents but was willing to play the long con? If I asked a question like that, he'd know I was on to him.

Oliver glanced over at me, and I flinched, training my eyes back on the road.

No. I knew him. I knew everything about him. So what if he had skills he hadn't shared with me? That didn't mean everything else I'd learned about him over the last year was a lie. Besides, I couldn't let myself think about this. I had to concentrate on formulating a plan. I had to figure out my next move.

"So...where're we going?" he asked. "What're we going to do?"

I pressed down on the accelerator, revving the engine. "We're going to find my parents. Wherever the hell they are."

18 MONTHS AGO

THE HOLLOW THUNK OF BULLETS HITTING THE MATTRESS AND embedding themselves in thick down registered in the back of my mind as my mother tackled me to the floor. Feathers rose up like fireworks around us, while glass rained over the gray carpet. My shoulder hit the ground first, then my temple, then my mother's weight settled over me. The Batphone slipped from her fingers and bumped across the floor, coming to rest near the foot of the bed.

The shooting stopped. Somewhere outside, brakes squealed. My mother groaned. I felt something warm trickle across my skin.

"Mom?"

She rolled over onto her back, her beautiful face contorted in pain. There was a hole in her sweater near her shoulder, and a thick stain was already spreading across her chest. But my mother was reaching for her leg. Another red stain blossomed on her shin.

"Mom! Are you all right?"

Dumb question, but it was a reflex. Clearly, she was not all right.

"Kaia, go back to your room!" she implored me, gripping the sleeve of my shirt in her hand. "Hide! You have to hide!"

"What? Mom, no. You're hurt. What can I do?" I shouted, tears brimming in my eyes.

"Nothing. There's nothing to be done. I need you to save yourself." Outside there were random shouts in Spanish. A dog barking. A church bell marked the hour with five mournful tones. "Go, Kaia! Run!"

"Mom, what's going on?" I pleaded.

"Listen to me, Kiki." My mother pulled me close, staring into my eyes. The sharpness in her eyes made my breath catch. "He's not coming back. Your father. He's gone, and he's never coming back."

chapter 6

KAIA

BLOND. I WAS ACTUALLY A BLOND. I HAD ALWAYS PROMISED MYSELF I would never dye my hair. I was happy with the way God had made me. My mom's hair and height, my dad's eyes and freckles. And now, if I bumped into them on the street, neither of them would recognize me.

I'd chopped off my hair at the chin and now I pulled it back into the shortest ponytail ever, hoping that would make me feel more normal. The red, rectangular glasses I'd bought at the drugstore along with the dye were a nice touch. I looked like one of the library hounds from school—the girls who wore graphic tees with oversized cardigans and held a weekly book club out in the courtyard. I'd always wanted to approach those girls. But if there was one life skill you didn't learn while globe-trotting with assassin parents, it was how to make friends.

Also, one of those girls had caught me talking to myself in the bathroom once—a habit I'd picked up over the many hours I'd spent by myself in strange hotel rooms—and I was pretty sure she thought I was insane.

I swiped the detritus from the dye box into the garbage. That was when I heard Oliver's voice. He was talking to someone. Quietly.

I'd gone through his phone while he was taking a shower. I wasn't proud of it, but I needed to check. There had been nothing unusual on it at all. A few missed calls from Robin and Brian and a couple dozen texts from them, which I hadn't read. There were no calls from unknown numbers, no cryptic outgoing texts, and all his contacts were names I recognized from school, plus a couple of social workers.

I'd been totally relieved. Until now. He hadn't told me he was going to call anyone. And it was after midnight.

Holding my breath, I took a step closer to the flimsy door that separated the crappy motel bathroom from the crappy motel bedroom.

"Yeah. A couple of days, I think," he said, then paused. "You never know with these things, I guess."

Who was he talking to? Robin? Brian? Or was it someone else? And what were "these things" he was talking about?

I opened the door, knowing his reaction would be my answer. But my jaw dropped. He was sitting on the bed, phone to his ear, surrounded by stacks of cash.

"I gotta go," he said before he set his phone aside. "That was Brian. I told him your grandmother was sick so he wanted to make sure everything was okay. Wow! You look completely—"

"Yeah, yeah, I know," I said, blushing as I tucked a stray

strand of hair behind my ear. "We'll get to that. But first, what the heck are you doing?"

Oliver looked around at the piles of bills. "Do you realize how much money this is?" he asked. "Fifty thousand dollars. Minus what we spent on gas and hair dye. Fifty thousand dollars!"

"Dude. Keep your voice down," I said, hugging myself. "The walls in this place are paper thin."

"Do you even understand what we could do with fifty thousand dollars?" he whispered.

"Yeah. We can pay for hotel rooms and gas and food until we figure out who the hell is trying to kill me and why."

I started to shove the money back into the bag. Oliver grabbed my wrist and rose up to his knees.

"Or." He raised his eyebrows suggestively. "We could get an apartment. Get jobs. We'd never have to go back."

"You, are crazy," I said with a laugh.

"No. I'm completely serious." He looped his arm around my waist and planted a long, firm kiss on my lips. "What the hell is there to go back to anyway? Out here it's just you and me. Are you really telling me you feel an overwhelming need to hang around Lockhart for another year of high school?"

"No, but you do," I said, shoving him off of me in a playful way. "What about soccer and your friends? What about your scholarship and college? What about Trevor? Why *wouldn't* you want to go back?" I asked, grabbing a few more stacks of money. "You're, like, the God of Lockhart High School. Your life is practically perfect."

Actually, his life was entirely perfect. If not for the fact that his mom was gone and his dad had ditched him, he had everything a kid could want. He loved his life. Aside from the occasional brooding moments about his parents and worrying about his autistic foster brother, Oliver was the happiest person I'd ever known.

"Whatever." He went quiet and sat down against the pillows, drawing the German's tablet toward him. "Forget I said anything."

My stomach felt hollow. What was wrong with me? Oliver was daydreaming about our future, and I had to go and be all realistic on him. I finished putting away the money and tossed the bag into the corner. Then I crawled onto the bed next to him and lay on my side, propped up on my elbow.

"Sorry," I said. "I guess I have a lot on my mind. But you are going to college next year, right? That's the plan."

"I guess," he said, not looking at me. He typed random numbers into the four-space password line over and over and over again.

"You are," I said, tugging the tablet out of his hand. "We both are." I cuddled against his chest and wrapped an arm around him. The glasses pressed uncomfortably against my face, so I took them off. "Well, as long as we don't get killed first," I joked.

"Exactly," he said under his breath.

But he didn't say it the way I'd said it. He didn't say it like he was joking, like he was trying to keep things light. He said it like he meant it.

chapter 7

OLIVER

EVERY INCH OF ME HURT, AND I'D ONLY BEEN DRIVING FOR AN hour. My eyes hurt from glancing from the rearview mirror to the road. My ankle ached from holding my foot at the exact same angle on the gas pedal. My shoulders and hands burned from gripping the wheel. My back and head throbbed from the tension of it all. Every time a car zoomed past us in the fast lane, I flinched. My armpits were stained with sweat and my hairline was wet with it too, and all I could think about was keeping Kaia from noticing how tense I was. Well that, and not getting pulled over by the highway patrol. I was probably the only person who could take apart a car and put it back together with no problem, but was terrified of actually driving one.

Because, technically, I didn't have a license. I had a learner's permit, but only because they offered classes through school. Robin had refused to pay for the test or take me to the DMV. Whenever I asked she'd say, "You don't have a car. Why do you need a license?" Deep down I was sure she was afraid that if I had a license, I'd steal her car and run, ditch the crappy situation the foster care system had dumped me in. And she might have been right.

Not that Kaia would have come with me if I bailed. We'd basically put that issue to bed last night. But I wasn't thinking about that now. I was thinking about whether the mattress that was tied to the car in front of us was going to fly off and hit our windshield.

Besides, whether or not Kaia would have left with me if I'd had the guts to steal a car didn't matter. We were here now. Free. What mattered was *keeping* her with me. Keeping us both alive. And not ever going back.

A black pickup truck leaned on its horn as it passed me and the gold Camry behind me, revving its engine like some kind of badass statement. God, what was wrong with people? I was doing the speed limit, loser.

The truck reminded me of Jack's truck though, and I wondered what kind of conniption fit Robin was having at this point. I'd turned off my phone last night after I talked to Brian specifically because I didn't want to be tempted to pick up her calls or read her texts. I knew how guilty she would make me feel, and I knew the guilt would mess with my head—make me consider going back. I wasn't about to let that happen. I'd made a decision. I'd chosen Kaia.

Except there was Trevor. I couldn't think about Trevor. He was my only weak spot in all this. The only person at home who really needed me. I used to think Kaia needed me. But now I wasn't entirely sure.

Kaia, meanwhile, seemed hyper alert and almost happy,

possibly because she was finally able to search the Internet. There had been no 4G signal at the motel, and when she'd tried to call her uncle Marco—who, it turned out, was her mother's brother—the number had gone straight to voice mail.

"Anything?" I asked, as she tapped away on her iPad.

Another three cars blew by us, and I tried to ignore them.

"Not a single news story." She glanced over at me, lips pursed. I still hadn't gotten used to the sight of her with blond hair. It made her eyes look like they were an entirely different color. Less blue and more gray. "How is a high-speed chase and shooting on the highway not front page news?"

"Maybe no one was paying attention?" I suggested. "Maybe the people who heard the gunshots thought they were fireworks or a blown tire?"

It wasn't entirely out of the question. People in our neighborhood were forever setting off fireworks, even in the middle of the damn day.

"Or someone is covering up the story." The way she said it made me feel naïve, but I didn't reply. Maybe I was naïve. Compared to her, I definitely was. So I kept my questions to myself and my eyes on the road.

"I'm putting in the first coordinates."

There was half a second of silence and then, "Oh my God."

"What?" I glanced at her and started to veer slightly off the road, then quickly yanked the wheel back, heart in my throat. She didn't even seem to notice.

"The coordinates. They're…"

Kaia trailed off and started humming. It took me a few bars to recognize the song, and when I did, I started to wonder if she was losing it. "Um, Kaia? Why are you humming the tune to *Elmo's World?*"

"Holy crap it is!" she exclaimed, then started tapping again.

"Can you please clue me in here?" I asked.

"What?" She looked up. "Oh, sorry. The first set of coordinates is the location of another one of my parents' safe houses. The one in Chicago. And the second coordinates..." She glanced at the screen. "It's for the safe house in upstate New York."

"What does any of this have to do with *Elmo's World?*" I asked as two school buses full of football players passed our car.

"When my parents taught me the addresses of these safe houses, I was really little. They put them to the tune of a familiar song so I'd remember them."

"Big Elmo fan, were ya?" I teased.

She shot me a scathing look as she typed in another set of numbers. "You weren't? Because that might be a relationship deal breaker."

I laughed. "Have I told you lately that you're adorable?"

"Gee, thanks," she said. Then she turned back to her iPad and back to business. At least I'd gotten her to crack a joke. That was something.

"What was this guy's deal?" she murmured. "How did he get all these locations? My parents and I were the only ones who knew where they were. They never even told Marco."

"So what does this mean?" I asked her.

"I have no idea," Kaia said. "Maybe if he didn't find me at Henry and Bess's he was going to check all of the safe houses to see if I was hiding out at one? Or maybe when he was done with me he was going to search these places for something else? Do you think he'd already been to the coordinates he'd crossed off? What else could he be looking for?"

"Money? Weapons?" I ventured.

Kaia shook her head. "I don't think so. If he's involved in some German crime syndicate, he'd have access to all that. It has to be something else."

"Like what?" I asked.

"I don't know. Maybe he was looking for proof that my parents pulled off the Hamburg job?"

"But why?" I asked. "What would he get out of proving your parents killed someone if they're already...you know—"

"Dead," she finished quietly. She squinted against the midday sun. "What if he was looking for my parents? He did ask me where my mother was. Maybe he thought she was hiding out at one of the safe houses."

I could hear the hope in her voice, and I knew I had to step lightly here. I didn't want to get her hopes up—or up even higher, I guess—but I also didn't want to kibosh them. Because what if it was true? What if she could get her parents back?

"Maybe," I said brilliantly.

She tilted her head, a blond lock falling over those sexy-librarian glasses. "What do you say we find out?"

I smiled. "Sounds like a plan."

My fingers curled tighter around the steering wheel, and I checked the rearview mirror.

The same gold Camry had been behind us for a while. I couldn't see the driver, but considering every other car on the road had felt the need to accelerate past our slow-moving vehicle, it was kind of weird that it was still behind us. At least there was no one in the passenger seat, which meant it wasn't the guys from the gas station. Scarface and his sidekick. Their mere appearance had scared the living hell out of Kaia.

I looked at the speedometer. Fifty-nine miles an hour. Crap. The limit here was fifty-five. I eased off the gas.

"Okay," I said, trying to keep my voice calm. "Where to?"

"We head to Chicago. Englewood to be exact. It was the first set of coordinates on his list, and I want to see if I can find what he was looking for."

I glanced at the rearview mirror again. The Camry was still there, the same distance behind our car as it had been for the last twenty minutes.

"Chicago? Awesome. I've always wanted to visit a big city."

My dad had sent me a birthday card from Chicago once, five years ago. At least, that was what the postmark had said. That card had included a twenty-dollar bill. He must have found a decent job there, at least for a while. My dad was in construction, an HVAC installation specialist, but he'd never kept a job for long. Back when my mom was alive, he used to try to stay close to where we were living—I guess she kept him in line, in a way—always reminding him he had a son he was supposed to be around for. But once she was gone, he'd barely lasted two weeks. I bet he loved the freedom to move from place to place, not always looking for a job within the same few counties among the same few companies. Clearly I wasn't enough to keep him rooted.

My throat was tight and I cleared it loudly. Screw my dad. It wasn't like he was still in Chicago. The last card, in March, had come from frickin' Albuquerque. But Chicago sounded cool. Maybe I could convince Kaia to stay there. I bet I could get work in a big city like that. Of course, Kaia was right: if I didn't go home, I'd have to give up on college. My early admissions application to UNC Charlotte was mostly filled out, and I was pretty sure I could get a scholarship, but it wasn't like that would happen if I didn't go back and finish out the season and then get my diploma. For so long I'd seen college as my ticket out, and I felt squirmy thinking about giving up on that goal.

Kaia stowed her iPad inside her backpack and toyed with her locket. She let out a long yawn before she spoke. "Chicago's not that big."

"No?" I asked.

"I mean, compared to other cities." She briefly lifted her shoulders.

"How many cities have you been to?" I asked.

"Oh, tons. New York, Boston, Houston, Miami, Paris, Marrakesh, Edinburgh, Tokyo, New Delhi. Honestly? If you want to see a big city, go to India. They're all big over there."

My stomach coiled into knots. I'd always thought Kaia was

a small-town kid like me. It was one of the things we'd bonded over. Occasionally, when I felt the need to be as far away from Robin's house as possible, I'd show up at Kaia's, and we'd go on adventures. At least, that's what we'd jokingly call them—our afternoon adventures. I'd take my bike, and she'd take her skateboard, and we'd ride from our little suburb into Charleston, then explore the old historical streets, making up stories about the people who used to live there. Sometimes we'd even break into one of the courtyard gardens and stare up at the stars through the blades of a palm tree, dreaming up plans for the future and all the places we'd go. The great thing about Kaia was she was never in a rush to get home. It seemed like our daydreams were a safe place. A place full of hope. An escape.

But she wasn't a small-town girl. She didn't need our afternoon adventures the way I did, because she'd been everywhere. She'd seen things I could never even hope to see. She'd traveled and experienced and lived. I suddenly felt like she'd been humoring me all that time. The poor foster kid who would never really go anywhere.

"What?" she asked, sitting up straighter. "What's wrong?"

"Nothing." I tried to shake off my jealousy and humiliation, along with this unsettling feeling that maybe I—a kid who'd never been outside the South Carolina state lines until today—wasn't enough for her, the wealthy daughter of ex-international spies-slash-assassins. "You must have thought I was so stupid, acting like riding my bike into Charleston was some big, exciting, like, voyage into the unknown or something."

"Oliver! I love our afternoon adventures. Do you have any idea what I would have been doing if we weren't out exploring? I'd be endlessly searching the Internet. Laying on my bed and wondering what had happened to my parents and whether I could have—"

She stopped and swallowed hard. "No. You have no idea how much all those times together meant to me."

We were quiet for a second. I wanted to believe her. But it didn't change the fact that she'd already been to half the places we'd planned to see together.

I glanced at the gold Camry again. It was still there.

"Well…how am I ever supposed to take you anywhere new if you've already been everywhere?" I asked.

Her brow furrowed as she turned in her seat, pressing her back to the window. She snapped her fingers. "California. I've never been to California," she said. "I've never seen the Pacific Ocean. From this side, anyway."

I laughed, the knot in my chest loosening. "Okay then. One day, before we die, I'm going to take you to California."

My eyes darted to the rearview. *Yep. Still there.*

"Why do you keep doing that?"

"Keep doing what?" I asked, stalling. I didn't want to worry Kaia. She'd had enough stress since yesterday.

"You keep looking in the mirror."

I could tell she wanted to check for herself but was forcing herself not to. Her whole body was rigid.

"There's a car," I said. "It's been there for a while now."

Kaia's skin went pale beneath her freckles. "Get off at this exit."

We were already approaching the off ramp. "What? Here?"

"Yes! Go! Now!"

"You want me to change lanes, just like that? Like—"

Kaia groaned, grabbed the wheel, and turned it. I hit the blinker and at the last second, we zoomed off the road and dipped down the ramp. I jammed the brake, slamming us against our seat belts and narrowly avoided crushing the car in front of us. I shot her a look, she shrugged, and then I eased to a more exit-worthy speed.

"Shit," Kaia muttered.

I glanced in the mirror. The car had followed us off the highway.

chapter 8
KAIA

WHEN OLIVER FINALLY PUT THE CAR INTO PARK, HE EXHALED LIKE a pilot who'd safely landed a 747 full of innocent people without his landing gear. He looked shaken, but I didn't have time to let him compose himself. A couple of cars had gotten between the Camry and our Honda on the local roads, but that would only buy us a minute or two.

"Come on. We have to move."

I shoved the door open, pulling my backpack with me—the Beretta tucked inside. We were on a side street in a town called Barton Mills, Kentucky. Pedestrians streamed by on the sidewalks, all headed toward Main Street, which was closed down due to something called "The Big 'Un BBQ Festival." Normally, I would have avoided a situation like this because of the traffic complications, but we needed to disappear into a crowd, and the crowd was on Main.

"Oliver!" I whispered desperately. "Let's go!"

He got out of the car at the same moment the gold

Camry parked illegally across the street, half-blocking a cross-walk. I cursed under my breath and ducked down, waiting to see who would get out of the car. In my mind's eye it was Scarface, twirling a silencer onto the end of a black .22, turning to aim at me with hard eyes. But it wasn't Scarface. It was a woman. Her brown hair was pulled into a bun, and she wore a camel leather jacket over torn jeans. She rose to full height and adjusted the jacket over her holster. She didn't look German and she didn't look Mexican. She had a more Nordic features—pale skin, high cheekbones. But who the hell really knew?

"What about our bags? The food?" Oliver asked.

"We'll come back for it if we can." Everything I really needed was in my backpack—iPad, cash, phone, gun—plus I had Jessica Martinez's ID in my jeans pocket and a knife in my jacket. I hated leaving Sophia behind, but I couldn't navigate this crowd on a skateboard. I walked around the car and grabbed Oliver's hand as the woman turned to look for us. "Don't turn around. Don't run. Walk. Fast."

We dodged in and out of foot traffic on the flower-lined sidewalk, making our way toward the police barricades set up across the intersection where the street met Main. Up ahead there were colorful tents, bobbing balloons, and clouds of smoke rising off the grills of a hundred barbecue pits. The air was filled with the delectable scents of sizzling meats and spicy rubs. Oliver and I dove into the crowd, milling around tables and lining up for beanbag tosses and bowling games. When my instincts said to hook a right, I went left instead. If I thought right, our newest stalker probably would, too.

"Do you have a plan?" Oliver asked.

"I'm trying to come up with one, but I'm suddenly starving." I told him.

"God, me too. Does it have to smell so good around here?" he asked, as a man in a white cowboy hat walked by us gnawing on short ribs.

The woman from the Camry appeared on the far corner, scanning the crowd. If she turned ninety degrees, she'd spot us.

"Over here."

I dragged Oliver across the sidewalk and into a brick alcove outside a large bank. We ducked into the corner, and I glanced out. Our pursuer paused in the center of Main Street, traffic parting around her as she blatantly studied each face that passed her by. The sun glinted off the mirrored sunglasses she'd pushed to the top of her head.

"Maybe we should split up," I said. "She's after me. I could try to draw her away and you could go back and get the car."

"And then what? How'm I supposed to find you again?"

Oliver had a point. Neither of us knew how to navigate this town, especially not with hordes of barbecue-eating pedestrians who'd taken over the street.

I peeked around the corner again. The woman's back was to us. Across the street, a restaurant with red awnings had three wide doors propped open to welcome in the public. I saw a man in a chef's hat walk out with a silver tray full of brisket and give it to one of the guys working the stands. He took an empty tray back inside with him.

Huh. Where there was meat, there were freezers. An idea came to me in a flash. My dad had once told me about a mission in Russia where he'd eluded a rival spy by using a freezer truck to his advantage. It had seemed so silly that I'd always wondered if he'd made it up as a bedtime story for me, but in this situation, it might actually work.

"Oliver?" I reached back and grabbed his hand. "I have a plan."

"Does it involve us eating chicken?" he asked, practically salivating as two girls with baskets of wings and fries strolled by the alcove. "'Cause that looks really—"

"If we pull this off, I'll buy you an entire bird," I promised him. "Now here's what you have to do."

———◄♥▻———

Oliver and I walked across the street, passing right through the sight line of our pursuer. I saw her flinch, and then we took off at a run, which wasn't easy. There were kids everywhere. Oliver tripped over a stroller and nearly took out a man hawking balloons. I was so busy helping him up, I didn't notice the woman with her yip-yip dog coming at us, and I momentarily got tangled up in its leash.

"Watch it, y'all!" The woman sneered, bending to scoop up her shaggy pup and standing squarely in our way.

I was about to snap at her when Oliver smiled. "Sorry about that ma'am," he said. I swear if he'd had on a ten-gallon, he would've tipped the brim.

The woman actually blushed. Then Oliver grabbed my hand and sidestepped her.

"You have a nice day!"

We were off again. Apparently a charming sidekick was an asset. It didn't hurt that he was gorgeous, too.

I glanced over my shoulder as we slipped inside the restaurant with the red awning out front. The Nordic chick had closed the gap between us big time. Clenching my jaw, I led Oliver toward the back of the restaurant. The tables were so jammed with diners, the servers so harried, the busboys so laden down with dirty dishes that they didn't even notice us breeze by. I pushed open the door to the kitchen and let Oliver in first. Before I ducked in after him, I caught a glimpse of a camel-colored jacket.

The back of the house was no different than the front. Four chefs worked the line, their hands blurred with movement. We moved along the wall, blending into the chaos.

At the rear of the kitchen, two hulking subzero freezers greeted us. One was propped open with a brick. I pulled Oliver behind a stack of empty glass crates and crouched down as the door pushed wider and a man emerged toting two huge sides of beef. He let the door slam shut.

"Okay. Stay here. Do not move until the time is right."

"Got it," Oliver said.

I started to stand, but he pulled me back and kissed me. Even in the insanity, my heart pitter-pattered when his lips met mine. I pulled away and smiled. "What was that for?"

"Just in case," he said, breathlessly.

"It's gonna be fine." *I hope.*

I got up and yanked open the door to the second freezer, then waited for the woman in leather. She caught sight of me, and I slipped inside, pretending to be startled—desperate. The walls were lined with shelves full of plastic vats, probably full of sauces and soups. The door hadn't even closed when she grabbed the handle and swung it wide open. The woman had beady eyes and a pointed chin. She didn't look like the type of person who was going to take any crap.

So many things could go wrong with my plan, and confronted by this woman, I instantly saw every one of them in vivid detail. She could shoot me. She could knock me out with a frozen pork loin to the skull. She could fight off Oliver. In fact, come to think of it, I didn't know how skilled Oliver was. That guy last night had gone down like a ton of bricks, but that could have been because he'd underestimated us. Or because Oliver had gotten in a couple of lucky kicks. What was I thinking?

Trying to look even more terrified than I felt, I backed to the wall. The air inside the freezer tightened my skin and made my breath cloud. I saw the moment the woman registered the fact that I'd backed myself into an actual corner—a glint lit up in her eyes like she'd never felt so lucky in her life.

"Rookie mistake." She pulled a .38 special from her holster and aimed it at my chest. This girl was old school. I had to respect that. With her other hand, she checked her phone, then narrowed her eyes at me. "You changed your hair."

"What?" I snapped. *What the hell was on that phone?*

"Look, I don't want to hurt you," she said. "So why don't you come quietly?"

"Who the hell are you?" I demanded.

I wanted answers. Did she know the German? Was she working with Scarface? Did she have the locations of my family's secret hideouts tucked in her passport as well? Who had sent all these crazies after me?

The woman tilted her head in a shrug. "Not important. Let's just say there are some people out there who will pay a lotta money to have you brought in."

"So you're a bounty hunter?" Silence. "Who hired you? Does this have to do with Oaxaca? Hamburg?"

"I don't know nothin' about Oaxaca or Hamburg." The woman sneered, contorting her features. "But wow, sure seems like your parents got around. You got other folks on your tail too?"

So it *was* about my parents. Not that there was ever any doubt. Her eyes narrowed as she leaned toward me slightly, the gun still steady. She took note of the scrapes on my face, the bruise on my head.

"Looks like someone worked you over in the last couple days." She seemed pleased. "I may have to up my fee."

She snapped my picture, then typed with her thumb.

"If you're going to make money off of me, the least you could do is tell me who sent you," I said.

"Like I'm gonna tell you that. Where's your little friend? He need a pee break or something?"

At that moment, Oliver stepped behind the woman and lifted his right foot. I dove out of the way as his heavy boot collided with the small of her back, sending her flailing forward, her gun and phone clattering to the floor. Turned out Oliver didn't need mad skills in this case, just the element of surprise. I grabbed the woman's gun, then brought my boot down on her hand as hard as I could. Her scream almost drowned out the crunch.

I raced past her and plucked her phone off the floor. Oliver dove out behind me and slammed the freezer door. Which had no handle on the inside, as I knew it wouldn't. The freezer was essentially a very cold prison cell.

"Did you really have to break her hand?" Oliver asked.

"You gotta do what you gotta do," I said.

He grimaced, and I grabbed his arm.

"What?" I demanded. "Are you hurt?"

"No. But now that she's mentioned it, I really do have to pee."

I rolled my eyes and hit a couple of buttons on the bounty hunter's phone. It hadn't locked yet. The picture she'd taken in the freezer was on the screen—I looked like a freaking zombie—and I deleted it. But the picture that popped up in its place made my blood run cold.

It was a shot of me and my mom. One I'd never seen before. We were both smiling as we held each other tight, cheek to cheek. It was how we always posed for photos when my dad was taking them—which was pretty much always. I had a purple streak in my hair, the same purple streak I'd had when we were in Oaxaca.

My dad never took pictures when we were on a job site, but he sometimes did before we left, or in the airport. He must have taken it when we were on our way to their last job. He'd never even had the chance to forward this to me. There was no way anyone could have this picture. Not unless they'd gotten ahold of my father's phone.

"Kaia? What is it? You look like you're gonna pass out."

Right then, the bounty hunter must've slammed her body into the heavy door. There was a thud followed by angry shouting. The words were so muffled by the heavy freezer door, I wouldn't have understood what she was saying unless I'd had a very good idea.

"Let's go," I said, shoving the phone into my pocket and pushing out into a dumpster-filled alley. No one in the kitchen was going to hear our captive, and if she had another gun on her, she couldn't shoot her way out without risking the bullet ricocheting back and hitting her. If the chefs were using the meat from the other freezer, it would be a while before anyone found her. I jogged to the end of the passageway with Oliver at my heels. There were plenty of people on the side street, but not as many as had been clogging Main. I walked to the next corner and ducked around the building.

"Are you gonna tell me what was on that woman's phone?" Oliver asked.

"Yeah, but first I'm gonna try something."

Hand shaking, I opened the bounty hunter's list of recent calls. The last five were all from the same number. Before I could double think it, I hit the callback button.

"What're you—"

I held a finger to my lips. Oliver sighed, but shut up. The line connected on the second ring.

"You got the girl?"

It was a woman. Clipped voice. Accent I couldn't quite place. "Yeah, I got her," I said. Oliver's eyes widened as he realized who I was talking to. "I'm calling for further instruction."

"George Bush Intercontinental. Get her there by ten p.m."

What. The. Fuck?

"Where're you taking her?" I asked, trying to keep my voice gruff. My mind was whirring, thinking three moves ahead, like my mom taught me when we played chess. Anticipate their next move and the one after that and the one after that. I thought of the hundreds of flights I'd taken over the years, the dozens of airports I'd waited in line in, eaten meals in, taken naps in.

"That's none of your concern."

"It is if you want me to drop her at the right terminal," I said.

There was a pause. A long one. I was caught. She was going to hang up.

"Air India," the voice said finally. "She's flying out on Air India. Our operative will meet you there with your payment."

The line went dead.

"Well?" Oliver asked. "What did they say?"

"Air India. They were going to take me to Asia." I looked at the phone's screen. I suddenly wanted to drop it on the ground and jump on it. Repeatedly.

"Shit. So first Germans, then Mexicans and now Indians? What the hell?"

"And look at this."

I brought up the picture of me and my mom and showed it to him, explaining its significance.

"How did some random bounty hunter get a picture that only your dad had access to?" he asked.

"I don't know. Maybe someone stole my dad's phone in Mexico? Someone who had a vendetta against my family?"

Was that what this was? Whoever'd killed my dad, then shot up our hotel room and killed my mom and thought they'd killed me had somehow realized I'd survived, and they were coming to finish the job?

Why had they taken my mom's body and not tried to take me? Why had they left me behind, only to come back for me now?

There was a loud peel of feedback from one of the stages at the Barbecue fest, and I jumped. An announcer drawled, "Welcome one and *y'all* to the twenty-first annual Big'Un Barbecue festival!"

A cheer rose from the street, and someone, somewhere, shot off a cannon.

"Let's move," I said.

I grabbed Oliver's hand, and we headed back toward the festival. I dumped the bounty hunter's phone in the first overflowing garbage can I saw. If she had GPS on the thing, I couldn't have her tracking us. Actually, shit. Why hadn't I thought about that before? I dug in my bag until I found the German's tablet and chucked that as well.

"What the hell?" Oliver said. "I spent like ten hours trying to hack that thing."

"Sorry. He could be tracking us with it."

"Oh, crap." Oliver's eyes widened, and he covered his mouth, glancing around as if Picklebreath was going to round the corner any second.

"God, I'm such an idiot," I said. "I should have ditched that thing the second we found it."

"Hey. It's okay. You were trying to figure out who's after us and why. It's totally understandable." Oliver put his hands on my shoulders, leaned in, and kissed the top of my head. "You, are anything but an idiot."

"Thanks." I allowed myself a half a second to lean into him. Okay, two or three seconds. "We should go."

"Yeah, but where're we going?" Oliver asked.

"First we find you a porta potty, then we get food, then we floor it."

"Sounds good," he said, tucking my hair behind my ear. "But you floor it. I'm done driving for a while."

"Whatever you say, Wingman."

Oliver grinned at the nickname, and together we lost ourselves in the crowd.

chapter 9

OLIVER

I NEVER SHOULD'VE TURNED ON MY PHONE. I'D DONE IT IN A moment of postbarbecue, full-bellied euphoria, thinking that having bested a badass bounty hunter, on a beautiful day like this, with my girl at my side, our situation couldn't be as horrible as I thought it could be. I was wrong.

We'd been back on the road for about an hour, Kaia behind the wheel, and I'd been staring at my cell phone screen for almost the entire time. There were a bunch of "Where U at?" texts from my friends and a few from my coach, which had left a knot in the pit of my stomach. I had a soccer game this morning, and there were going to be college scouts there—some of them looking to meet me. I'd never missed a game before unless it was for a broken bone. But missing the scouts was the least of my problems. There were dozens of texts and missed calls from Robin in the last twenty-four hours. I didn't listen to the voice mails, but the texts were unavoidable. Once I started reading, I couldn't stop. The first few were seminormal.

> your 5 mins late 4 curfew
> shouldnt u b home by now?
> where r u? DO I HAVE 2 CALL THE COPS???!!!

Her tone gradually descended into guilt-slinging hysterical.

> U BEST NOT HAVE RUN OUT ON US
> WHAT ABOUT TREVOR? U ONLY EVER THINK ABOUT URSELF.

I gripped the phone so tight my fingers hurt. I was so mad I wanted to throw the thing out the window, until I remembered how much it had cost me.

> ITS THE MIDDLE OF THE NIGHT!!! IM CALLING THE COPS.
> I AM. U HAVE 3 MINS TO WALK THRU THAT DOOR OLIVER
> I SWEAR TO GOD

But she hadn't called the cops. She wouldn't. Because that would have brought attention to her. To her family. Her household. Her estranged husband, his drug habit, and his violent tendencies. So I was pretty sure she hadn't called them. The next few texts were calmer.

> WHERE R U? CALL HOME.
> come home oliver. itll b different i swear.
> trevor misses u. he was confused when he woke up and
> u werent here. broke my heart.

At least none of Robin's messages mentioned a visit from Jack. If he'd been there, she wouldn't have been able to resist telling me, laying that responsibility on me. So I knew that Trevor was all right. For the moment. I took a breath and typed a response. It took a minute, because my fingertips were so sweaty.

be back soon.

No. That was a straight-up lie. I looked at the trees zooming by outside the windows as Kaia drove us through Indiana. I didn't even know exactly where I was, but I knew I wasn't going back to South Carolina anytime soon. I deleted the text.

God, poor Trevor. That kid already had so much to deal with, between his special school and being teased by kids in the neighborhood. I'd left him to deal with his father too. I'd left him without a buffer between him and a mom who had no clue how to protect him.

i'm sorry…

No. I wasn't going to apologize. I hadn't done anything wrong. Not really. They weren't my family. Trevor was not my responsibility. He was Robin's. Maybe leaving them would force her to finally realize that. And besides, she'd abandoned me a hundred times over in a hundred different ways. She didn't love me. So why shouldn't I take off? Why *shouldn't* I disappear with the one person in the entire world who actually cared that I existed?

I looked at Kaia. I couldn't believe she was still functioning. It was pretty clear that someone was after her in a big way, but why? I wished I knew more about her history, her parents. Then maybe I could help her figure out that mystery. If only she'd told me from the beginning—who she really was, where she was really from—I hated that there was so little I knew about my girlfriend when I'd thought I knew everything.

Until Kaia shared every last detail of her life, she was on her own when it came to constructing the conspiracy theories portion of this drama, and the strain was clear on her face. Besides, it wasn't like she knew everything about my life. Not by a long shot. I deleted the text.

i'm fine. Will be in touch when I can.

There. Make it about me. That would shock the crap out of her. If she even picked up on it.

"Who're you texting?" Kaia asked.

"No one." I deleted the text and shut off my phone. My face sizzled with anger, sadness, and guilt. I shoved the phone deep into the pocket of the black jacket I'd been wearing on and off since we left the safe house, though right then I was so hot it was making me itch. I reached over and flicked on the air conditioning.

"You're not telling them where we are, are you?" Kaia asked, tense.

"What? No. Who would I tell?"

"I don't know. Robin…Hunter…Brian…someone."

Someone? Who the hell was someone? And why was she saying it in that weird, leading voice?

"Well, I'm not texting anyone. No one would believe where I was anyway," I told her.

"Good, because if people start asking around, they'll figure out you're with me, and if they know you're with me, they'll start asking the people you know where we are, and it's better for them if they don't know anything."

My nerves crackled. "Wait, you don't think someone's going to come after Trevor and Robin, do you? Like they did Bess and Henry?"

Kaia had tried calling Bess and Henry again after lunch. Still no answer.

Kaia's face said it all, but her answer contradicted her expression. "No. No. Of course not."

"Shit." I said, my palms starting to sweat.

"Oliver, I'm sure they'll be fine. But…"

"But what?"

"But, if you want to go home…"

For a half a second, I considered it. Yes, I wanted to get the hell out of Robin's, but I'd always thought that the most reasonable and realistic way to do that was to keep my head down, get good grades, maybe land a partial athletic scholarship, take out some loans, and go to college. I'd already missed one important game. If I missed another… And we had a history paper due next Friday. And all those chem labs… Shit. I'd survived as long as I had under Robin and Jack's roof. All I had to do was survive another ten months and I would be free.

"What're you thinking?" Kaia asked.

I looked at her. At the cuts on her face, the bruise on her forehead, the question in her blue eyes. And my doubts melted away. I couldn't abandon her now.

Maybe I could at least warn Robin. Maybe she would take Trevor to her mom's or something. Then he'd be safe from Kaia's crazy stalkers *and* Jack. And I could tell Robin to call the school and say I was sick—like really sick—and might be out for the week. Just to keep the door open...

"You *can* go home. If you want to," Kaia finished.

Great. Now she was trying to get rid of me. Had I not proven I was worth having around?

"Well, I want to be with you," I told her gruffly. "I kind of thought you knew that, but whatever."

"I'm sorry," Kaia said. "I didn't—"

"Forget it. It's fine."

I crooked my arm on the door and leaned my head into my hand. I couldn't stop thinking about Trevor. Yesterday, when I'd left to pick up Kaia, I'd told him I'd play Battleship with him when I got home and he'd given me a rare smile. I imagined him sitting at that little table in his room all night, the Battleship set ready to go, waiting for me. Waiting for me and I'd never shown up.

I pulled the jacket's hood up over my face.

"Are you okay?" Kaia asked.

I didn't answer. I didn't trust my voice not to crack.

"Oliver?"

I cleared my throat. "M'fine."

I could feel her watching at me, but I stared out the window. I didn't want her to see my watery eyes, the red blotches that were definitely growing across my cheeks.

"All that barbecue made me tired, I think."

"Or you're coming down from the adrenaline," Kaia said. "After a close call like that, it's normal to crash, you know?"

She leaned forward over the wheel so she could see me, and gave me this funny look, like my answer really mattered.

"Not really. I've never been on the run before."

But I did know. I'd had my fair share of last-second escapes.

"I'm gonna try to take a nap," I told her.

"'Kay," Kaia said quietly.

I leaned my head against the passenger door, closed my eyes, and tried like hell to make myself stop thinking.

◁ ❤ ▷

A truck horn blared and I woke up gasping for breath, instinctively bracing for the impact. But the car wasn't moving. My mouth was gummy, and my head felt heavy. The sun bore down on me, turning the black jacket into a private sauna. I unzipped it and looked around.

Rest stop. Tons of cars. And no Kaia. I blinked and stared at the silver key chain stamped with some kind of intricate Gaelic-looking symbol that dangled from the ignition. There was money on the passenger seat. I couldn't make what I was seeing make sense.

Had someone driven up behind us and forced us off the road? Had the money fallen out of her bag when they'd grabbed her? Where was she? What the hell had I slept through?

I grabbed the keys, shoved the money in my back pocket—because, hello, invitation to break in—and got out of the car, leaving the jacket on the front seat. The mid-September sun was high in the sky, and waves of heat rose up off the tarmac by the gas pumps where several tractor-trailers waited in line. I scanned the cars, the faces of the weary travelers as they passed, searching for Kaia or anyone suspicious.

Where was she? What if something had happened to her?

Terror swelled in my chest. My fingers curled around the key chain. I stopped when I reached the paved sidewalk around the white building, where a sign in the window advertised *EGG SPECIAL! $2 (plus tax)*, and a family of five had to step down onto the asphalt to walk around me. I turned in a slow circle, the heat and the mounting panic making my vision blur.

My mother had already been taken from me. Not Kaia too.

I headed inside the building and slammed into a linebacker type with a long beard and dark sunglasses. His monster-sized soda spilled over the rim of the cup and onto his arm and splattered my still bloody shoes.

"What the hell!? Watch where you're going, son!"

"Sorry," I muttered, skirting around him.

From the way he followed me with his eyes, watching me go

through the door, I half expected he was going to follow me and crush my skull. But when I glanced back, he was shaking soda off his wrist and heading for a red pickup. I was hit with a sudden wave of nausea. What if he'd taken Kaia? What if she was tied up in the bed of that truck? I almost ran after him, but the man was already peeling out of the parking lot and gunning it for the highway. I backed up toward the wall, dozens of people eating ice cream, buying candy bars, streaming for the bathrooms, and felt light-headed.

I had no clue how long I'd been asleep. Kaia could be curled up in the trunk of any one of these trucks or cars. She could be halfway to Mexico by now. I'd failed her. Why the hell had I fallen asleep? Had I really lost the love of my life because I was feeling sorry for myself? Because I'd needed to take a *nap*?

I forced myself to breathe, and as I did, our last conversation came back to me in bits and pieces. Kaia suggesting that I might want to go home. Her hinting that maybe she even wanted me to go home.

Keys in the ignition. Money on the seat. I pulled the bills out of my pocket, turned toward the wall for a little privacy, and counted it. A thousand dollars. *A thousand freaking dollars*. It was more cash than I'd ever held in my hand at one time. I shoved it away, glancing around to make sure no one had noticed. There wasn't a single soul looking at me. All these people were roaming around, and I was totally invisible. No one had a clue where I was, and in a hot flash of panic, I realized that no one cared.

Shit. *Shit!*

Bracing my hands above my knees, I leaned forward and sucked in air.

"Oliver?"

I straightened and waited for the head rush to pass. Kaia was standing not five feet away, her backpack and skateboard strapped to her back, holding an iced coffee in one hand and a Red Bull in the other. My body flooded with relief.

"You woke up," she said. But she didn't smile. She looked sort of…distressed. Obviously she was distressed. This was a distressing trip. I was so glad to see her I almost mowed down a toddler to throw my arms around her.

"I got you a Red Bull," she said into my shoulder.

Red Bull, my third favorite.

"I thought you were gone," I breathed.

She wrapped her arms around my back, holding the drinks away from me, then pulled back.

"Where would I go?" she asked with a wan smile. "We're in this together, right?"

She searched my face like she was looking for the meaning of life. I felt this odd hitch in my chest, as if I'd done something wrong. Maybe she *was* mad at me for falling asleep, for leaving her to drive all that time with no one to talk to. Maybe that's why she had bought so much caffeine, as a hint. I resolved to try to be better. I'd prop my eyelids open with toothpicks if I had to.

"Yeah," I said. "We're in this together."

18 MONTHS AGO

"MOM!? TELL ME WHAT TO DO! CALL 911? DO THEY HAVE 911 in Mexico?"

Grunting and gasping, my mother pushed herself up on one elbow, then into a seated position, letting out an awful wail of pain. She slumped back against the side of the bed, heaving for breath. I looked into her eyes to keep myself from staring at the blood. There was so much blood.

"Kaia, listen to me, you have to run."

"Mom, no. You have to tell me what's going on. What do you mean, dad's never coming back?"

"The phone."

My mother gestured weakly at the Batphone. I scrambled to it on my knees and grabbed it. The screen displayed one word, all lowercase letters: run

"It's code. He's compromised."

"Compromised? I don't understand."

"We never should've come here," my mom said. "I knew it.

I told him. But does he ever listen to me? No. One last job. One last job and then..."

My pulse pounded in my ears. "One last job? Mom, what are you talking about? Please tell me what's going on. I don't—"

My childish rambling was cut short by the sound of car doors slamming. One, then two, then three and four, right outside the exterior door to our room. My mother gasped. "He's found me."

When I looked down at her, her eyes had gone unfocused as if staring at something in the distance.

"Oh, God. He's found me."

chapter 10

KAIA

WE CAUGHT MORE THAN A FEW CURIOUS GLANCES AS I PULLED THE car alongside a crumbling curb in Chicago that evening, possibly because every other car we'd seen for the past three blocks had either been dented, had windows smashed in or was half rusted-out. The sun was starting to set, and shadows loomed across the pavement. Half the homes on the street were boarded up, and the chain link fences were overgrown with weeds and vines. A man shuffled his way down the sidewalk clutching a bottle inside a brown paper bag. A siren shrieked nearby, followed by the sound of breaking glass.

"For a safe house, it doesn't seem to be in the safest neighborhood," Oliver said. He looked worried.

"Sometimes places like these are the best camouflage there is," I told him, paraphrasing something I'd once heard my father say when we were holed up in a shady district in Oslo. I shoved open the driver's side door and pulled my backpack straps over both shoulders. "Let's go check it out."

I took out my skateboard and dropped it on the sidewalk,

my feet practically itching for a ride. Before I got on, I reached for Oliver, lightly entwining my fingers with his. When he squeezed my hand, I told myself for the hundredth time that I'd done the right thing by not ditching him. I'd come close—leaving the money on the seat, the keys in the ignition, hoping he'd take the hint and head for safety—but the second I saw that Red Bull display in the convenience store, I realized what a jackass I was being.

I loved him. And I needed him. I didn't give a crap if he *was* some babysitter hired by my parents. And if he'd started out a bad guy, then maybe he'd fallen in love with me and been turned good by my irresistible wiles. I'd read hundreds of books, so I knew this was at least somewhat possible. What really mattered was, aside from Henry and Bess, Oliver was the only person who had been there for me this last year. That had to mean something.

If it wasn't for Oliver, I'd probably still be sleeplessly haunted by nightmares. It was Oliver who had spent an entire month up late on the phone with me, talking in low tones, telling me silly stories until I dozed off. It was Oliver who had done all the research on insomnia and taken me for long walks in the sun at lunch and insisted on afternoon adventures, knowing that exercise and fresh air would help me sleep at night. He'd sacrificed a lot to help me: all-important cafeteria time with his uberpopular friends, after-school hours when he could have been studying, his own rest—and I appreciated it more than he'd ever know.

The sidewalk was uneven and weedy, so I rolled slowly, keeping pace with Oliver as he walked.

"One-twenty-one, right?" Oliver said, looking up at the nearest house. Its blue siding was moldy in spots and completely missing in others. "There's no number on this one."

"There," I said, pointing at a leaning mailbox. "One-seventeen."

One-twenty-one was a two-story red brick building with white trim that had seen better days. The gate hung open, and the small, square front yard was nothing but a dirt patch peppered with crushed beer cans, random food wrappers, and one headless baby doll. I tamped down a quivering unease in my gut, hopped off the board, and popped up the lead wheels to grab them. Then I lead the way up the creaking stairs and went to the second window to find the key. There was nothing there.

Had the German been here? Had he found the keys? Why didn't I search his bag better?

Something tickled the back of my neck, and I whirled around.

"What? What's wrong?" Oliver positioned himself near the front door, his jacket zipped to his chin against the quickly dropping temperature.

"Nothing. Just got the weirdest feeling that someone was watching me."

Clutching Sophia in one hand, I looked from window to window across the street, but there wasn't so much as a porch light on, let alone lights inside the houses. I saw no one. Nothing. For some reason, that made me feel even more nervous. Somewhere in the distance a dog barked frantically, and I had a vivid memory of blood on my skin and my mom's labored breathing.

"Kaia?" Oliver asked worriedly.

I blinked back to the present. "There's no key."

Oliver reached for the door handle and turned it. The door swung open with an ominous creak. Holding my breath, I stepped up next to Oliver and peered inside. The house was dark, the gray light of dusk barely permeating the drawn curtains. An awful, stale stench wafted out at us, and I wrinkled my nose, leaning through the doorframe.

A chill skittered down my back. There it was again. That feeling that we weren't alone.

"Hello?"

There was a rustle, like an animal running through dry leaves, and a woman burst toward me as if from nowhere, her eyes wide and shot through with red veins. I threw my board up to defend myself, but it was too late. She barreled right into me, knocking me onto my ass on the front stoop, before waddle-running down the steps and taking off on the sidewalk. Sophia went flying and clattered against the porch rail.

"Kaia!" Oliver crouched next to me. "Are you okay?"

My heart pounded in my throat. Aside from a sore butt and a bruised ego, I was fine. "Nothing's broken," I muttered.

Satisfied, Oliver jumped to his feet. "Hey! It's okay! Come back!" he shouted after the woman.

"What're you doing?" I demanded.

"I feel bad," he said, lifting his palms. "She probably just needed a place to stay, and we scared the crap out of her."

I squeezed his hand. "Sometimes you are too sweet to comprehend."

Oliver watched after the woman, but it was clear she had no intention of returning and making friends. He took a tentative step inside the house. "Yep. Looks like she was squatting."

I blew out a breath, straightened myself up and dusted myself off, feeling more rattled than I'd ever admit. How was I supposed to get through this if I let a harmless woman startled out of her sleep throw me off my game?

I checked on Sophia, who was fine—she's a tough girl—and decided to leave her on the porch to keep my hands free for any more sudden attacks. Steeling myself, I followed Oliver inside. The living room was a trashed mess. Two couches had been pushed against the walls and in the center of the room was a large, blackened scorch mark, where someone had clearly set a fire. Remnants of blackened newspaper were strewn everywhere. Some of the curtains had been burned at the edges, and another scorch mark tarnished the far wall, where a door led to a dingy kitchen at the back of the house. There was detritus all over the floor, from paper bags to vodka bottles to crack pipes and needles. A bureau had been toppled over and the doors ripped off, probably for firewood. In one corner lay a pile of newspapers and blankets so big, I briefly wondered if someone else was hiding under them, until Oliver went over and toed at it, scaring up one gray rat, but nothing else.

"Ugh. I hate rats," Oliver said with a shudder.

I sidestepped as the rodent raced by. "Looks like the neighborhood has taken over in more ways than one."

"Don't get me wrong, I know this is your family's place and all, but we're not staying *here*, right?" Oliver asked.

I walked past him toward the kitchen. "Yeah, no. Let me take a quick look around. I want to see if we can figure out what the German was looking for."

It was wishful thinking that my parents might have been here. That they might have left me some clue as to what had happened, where they were. Even if they had, it was possible that the German had found it and taken it. Or that someone else had—like that random woman who'd knocked me on my butt. But that odd feeling I had on the front stoop spurred me forward. It felt like I was supposed to be here, that there was something here that I was meant to find.

I pulled open a few drawers and rummaged through spoons and plastic knives, unopened squares of wet naps. A search of the cabinets yielded nothing except expired canned corn, rat droppings, and a pair of large cockroaches. On the counter near the broken down refrigerator I found a pile of papers—take-out menus with coffee rings, a list of football teams with scores and dollar amounts listed next to each one. When I tossed the pile back onto the counter, a photo fluttered out.

Oliver bent to pick it up before I could. "Is this you?"

I walked to his side and leaned into his shoulder. My breath caught in my lungs. It was an old, creased photo of me in the park near my house in Houston. Both my parents were behind me, laughing as they pushed me on the swing. My smile was so wide it had all but closed my eyes. There were so few pictures of the three of us, this was like finding pure gold.

"Yeah, that's me." I took the photo from him gingerly, my heart growing with each pump of blood until it filled my ribcage. It was as if I could hear my mother's laughter clear as a bell inside my mind, then my father's low chuckle. "And my parents."

"How old are you in that?" he asked.

"Four, I think."

I didn't remember the day the picture was taken, but I recognized the pink sweater I was wearing. I'd worn that thing until it was basically a crop top with holes in the elbows. My mother had finally tossed it when I was six, even though I begged her not to. It looked new in the picture.

Oliver gave me an earnest, understanding smile. He only had a few pictures of him and his mom, none with his father. I had some photos of my parents on my iPad—and now the one on the bounty hunter's phone—but nothing this old.

"Cute kid," he said.

I smiled. "Thanks."

How had this photo gotten here? Had one of my parents left it behind by mistake? Or as some kind of clue? And if so, when? What did it mean?

The photo was small enough to slide into the back pocket of my jeans with the passport, without folding it. I wanted to keep it close. I looked around at the dingy windows, the broken cabinets, the grimy floor, and felt myself deflate.

Where the hell are you? I thought, my insides clenching. *What is going on?*

There was no answer, other than a creak of floorboards overhead. Oliver and I both flinched.

"What's that?" he asked, looking past me.

I turned. There was a red wire sticking out from underneath the door of what might have been a pantry. I stepped closer, held my breath, and yanked on the handle. The wire was old and dusty with two cut ends. The gold threading frayed out from inside the plastic coating. I would have walked away, except there were fresh footprints in the thick layer of dust on the pantry floor. I peeked further inside, and saw a red light blinking overhead and a black box affixed to the ceiling.

Bomb!

I grabbed Oliver's arm, but he stepped past me.

"Oliver, don't!"

He lifted onto his toes, inspecting the box.

"What're you—"

"I think it's a security system," he said.

My heart paused its hammering. "What?"

He dropped back down to his heels. "We have one like it at the shop. Hang on." He took out his phone and shone the light on the box. "Yeah, the wires go through here."

Oliver slid past me into the kitchen and opened the next cabinet. "They go through here…" He opened the cabinet. "And here…" He kept opening doors until he came to the sink and looked up. "Yep. There it is. That's the tiniest camera I've ever seen."

"Oliver!" I whispered as I hit the floor, dragging him with me. His shoulder hit the edge of the countertop as he came down.

"What?" he asked. "And also, ow."

"Sorry," I said through my teeth. "But what if the German left it? What if his cronies are watching the feed? Maybe that's why he came here—so he could install surveillance—and now they know where we are!"

"Crap. Sorry. I figured your parents probably put it in."

"Maybe," I said. "But I doubt it would still work. There's no power in this place and the battery would have run out by now. Right?"

"Unless it's some kind of super-awesome, spy-grade battery," Oliver said, nudging me with his elbow.

"True…"

"I was kidding," Oliver said.

If my parents installed the camera, did that mean they'd wired all the safe houses? And if so, why? Did they think they'd been compromised? Well, they definitely had now, considering the German and presumably whomever he worked for knew exactly where they all were.

My fingers curled into fists. This wasn't right. This was

supposed to be a safe place—somewhere we could go when we were in trouble. It belonged to my family. And the very idea that it had been violated seriously pissed me off.

I glared at the camera. I wanted to tell whoever was watching to fuck off, but cameras that small didn't necessarily have audio capabilities.

"Kaia! What are you doing?" Oliver whispered.

"I'm sick of running. And I'm sick of not knowing what's going on." I rummaged through the drawers until I found a pen, then flipped over a piece of scrap paper and wrote my own note.

> Whoever you are, we need to talk.
> (817) 555-9113

I underlined my number three times, then held it up to the screen and counted silently to ten Mississippis. Then I crumpled the paper into a ball and threw it into the sink.

"Let's bail," I said. "I don't like this place."

We stepped into the living as two men stepped in through the front door. One of them was tall with dark skin marked by patches of pink, and wiry hair that was spotty in places. His jeans were too baggy, and his shirt was too tight. He twitched at the sight of us. The other man was short but broad with hair like straw and a scraggly yellow beard. His eyes seemed to roll around of their own accord, refusing to focus. He wore three jackets layered on top of each other and cargo pants cut off six inches above the ankle. They were both carrying tattered brown shopping bags, softened by age, and the smaller one clutched Sophia by one of her axels. More squatters.

I was already angry. Seeing some guy manhandling my board pushed me over the edge. For a second, there was a High Noon-worthy standoff. Then, the tall man stepped forward.

"Watchu doin' in our house?" he demanded. His voice was far too loud for the small space.

Honestly, it was all I could do to keep from launching myself at him Spider-Man style, but Oliver, levelheaded wonder that he is, jumped in.

"Sorry man. We got the wrong place. We were just leaving."

"You got no right to be here," the man accused, his nostrils flaring. "Get out!"

"That's exactly what we're going to do," Oliver said in a soothing voice. "Kaia?"

"But he's got my—"

"*Kaia.*"

Oliver tugged my backpack and edged around the men in a wide circle, keeping his back to the wall. I did the same. More than anything, I wanted to grab Sophia, but even through the blinding adrenaline I knew that would be a very stupid idea. The tall man followed us with his gaze. The two of them were so close to the door that we were going to have to squeeze out behind them if they didn't move.

Oliver paused. The man who had stolen my board finally focused—on me. He looked me up and down like I was a piece of finely seasoned meat.

"Excuse me," Oliver said to the taller man, gesturing for him to let us pass. "If you wouldn't mind—"

Out of nowhere, the man hauled off and punched Oliver in the stomach. I shouted in surprise as Oliver doubled over, his hand flying out to brace himself on the wall. I reached for him as the other man dropped Sophia with a clatter, grabbed both my elbows, and pulled them behind me, dragging me back toward the kitchen while I kicked and writhed. The weight of the knife was heavy in my jacket pocket, but I couldn't get to it with my arms pinned behind me. I watched helplessly as the tall man kneed Oliver's chin.

"Oliver!" I screeched.

The man holding me smelled like rotten eggs and tuna. He cackled when Oliver hit the wall.

"You're comin' with me, girlie," he growled, and I felt something wet flick my ear. His tongue.

Dammit to hell. I tipped my head forward and jerked it back as hard as I could. The room exploded in stars as the back of my skull collided with my attacker's cranium and my fake glasses hit the floor. He let go of me and staggered sideways, crushing the frames under his heavy boot. So much for that element of my disguise. I lunged to help Oliver as he landed a right hook across the tall man's face. The crack was followed by a spurt of blood. It seemed Oliver could handle himself.

The blond man grabbed my arm. I gripped his elbow and twisted, bringing him to his knees. Near the door, Oliver's adversary threw punches, only a few of which landed. It almost looked as if Oliver was humoring the guy—giving him a sporting chance.

"Mercy!" my guy wailed dramatically "I call mercy!"

"What are we, in fourth grade?" I demanded. "You *licked* my *ear!*"

"I'm sorry! I didn't mean to!"

I rolled my eyes, then slammed him with a fist to the temple. He went down on his stomach, his eyes closed, kicking up a cloud of dust. Behind me, wood splintered. I turned to find Oliver was in a headlock. How the hell had that happened? I was about to grab a two-by-four from a pile of splintered wood, but Oliver suddenly bent forward, throwing the guy over his shoulder with a grunt and landing him flat on his back on the dirty floor.

The tall man groaned. The blond man let out a gurgling sound. Oliver shot me a self-satisfied smile. It died the instant he saw my face.

This was not normal. If he could throw moves like that, why didn't I know about it? Why would he have kept this a secret from me?

"What?" he asked.

The adrenaline got the better of me. I couldn't stop myself.

"Enough is enough," I said. "Who the hell *are* you?"

chapter 11

OLIVER

THE ACCUSATION AND PAIN IN KAIA'S EYES KILLED ME. I TURNED and stormed out of the house, speed-walking down the street, blowing right past our car. The sun had set and the sky was an inky purple-blue. I kept walking across the street and into another equally run-down neighborhood.

What kind of question was that? "Who the hell *are* you?" Like I was the one who'd been lying about my past, my parents, my grandparents, where I came from. She'd made up an entire story for herself, and you didn't see *me* jumping all over her case. And hadn't *I* saved our asses back there? Where did she get off questioning me?

Shit. What was I doing here? I'd missed meeting scouts for this? Suddenly I became very aware of the thousand dollars in my back pocket. I wondered if she'd even miss it. Did she even realize it had fallen out of her bag? I could go home. Get my life together before it fell completely apart. Hell, I'd taken out two guys in two days. Maybe the next time Jack came for a visit I'd actually have the stones to try my moves out on him.

Up until now, every time I thought about really standing up for myself, for Trevor, I'd chickened out. Well not again. Never again.

I'd pay Kaia back for the loan as soon as I could. If I ever saw her again.

"Oliver! Wait up!"

I heard her wheels on pavement and knew she'd catch up to me in seconds, but I kept walking. I crossed another street. On the next block, the streetlights were working. There was a chill in the air now that the sun was going down, and I yanked my jacket's zipper to my chin.

"Oliver, please." Kaia stumbled off her board and tugged on my arm, trying to make me face her. I stared stoically off in the direction I'd been walking. "I'm only saying!" Kaia pleaded, her palms out. "Last week the most athletic thing I'd seen you do was score a winning goal on a header, and now suddenly you're Jackie Chan? Enough with the secrets, Oliver. Tell me who you really are. I swear I won't be mad. I just want to know."

"Why do you keep saying that?" I bit out. "'Who I really am?' I'm just me. I'm not gonna morph into an alien or something."

She shifted her weight and stared at me, frustrated. "Why do you know how to fight like that? How do you wake up one morning and know karate?"

"I *didn't* wake up one morning and know how to do it, all right?" I spat. "I've been studying jujitsu for three years."

Kaia blinked. "What?"

"You know that guy from calc? Leo Goto?" I shoved my hands deep into the pockets of my jacket.

"Yeah…"

"Well, his family is all math geniuses, but he hardly got past eighth-grade algebra, so we bartered. I've been tutoring him in math, and he's been giving me jujitsu lessons."

Kaia's brow creased like she was working through a particularly hard SAT word problem. "How did I not know this?"

"I don't tell you every little detail either," I said. "We crammed the math in during study hall, and he'd coach me after my shifts at the store. I've been telling you and Robin my closing shifts at the shop went an hour later than they actually did so that we could go to his place and spar."

"Okay," Kaia said slowly. Clearly she was trying to process this. "But why would you keep that a secret?"

I let out a short laugh and covered my face with my hands. My whole body throbbed with the effort of holding in the truth. "I just did, okay?"

"Why?" she demanded.

I started walking again.

"Oliver, what's going on? Tell me!" Kaia said. "Oliver, please—"

She touched my arm again and I whirled around. "I kept it a secret because if Robin found out she would make me stop."

Kaia blinked. "But why would she—"

"Because she doesn't want me to fight back! I'm *that kid*, all right!?" I blurted. "The pathetic foster kid whose fake father uses him as a punching bag!"

To my horror, a tear spilled onto my cheek. I wiped it away

as fast as I could, but it was too late. The pressure in my chest had welled up into my throat and was cutting off my air supply.

"What?" Kaia breathed.

"All the bruises, Kaia? The ones I told you were from soccer and lacrosse?" I said, my voice cracking. "They're not. They're from him! Yeah, Robin threw him out, but he still comes by and usually only when he's been on a bender. The first time...a few years ago...he came after Trevor and I got in his way. And the time after that and the time after that... Now he comes after me. Every time. Only me."

"Oliver...oh my God." She reached for me, but I angled away. "Why didn't you tell me?"

My jaw clenched. I could see the pity in her eyes. The sorrow. Five minutes ago she might have thought I was keeping secrets, but at least she thought I was strong. Her wingman. Someone who could protect her, who wasn't a liability, who was worth having on this little adventure of hers. Now she saw me for what I really was: a pathetic little kid whose father abandoned him. A loser who took beatings on a regular basis. I was nothing but an orphan who no one loved.

"You're one to talk about keeping secrets," I said bitterly.

Then I turned around and kept right on walking.

chapter 12

KAIA

MY HEART BROKE OPEN. THERE WAS SO MUCH HURT IN OLIVER'S eyes. And I hadn't seen it because I'd only been thinking about myself. I'd only considered his existence as it pertained to me. When the hell had I become so freaking self-centered? Suddenly all I wanted was to drive back to Charleston, find this asshole foster father of his, and give him the same treatment I'd given Picklebreath. But he was there, and we were here, and Jack didn't matter anymore. Oliver had gotten away from him, and he was never going back—not if I had anything to say about it. Our future was all that mattered.

And now he was walking away from me. I'd made my own worst nightmare come true.

"Oliver!" I shouted. "Oliver, wait!"

Right then, my phone beeped and my heart stopped. No one had this number other than Oliver, Henry, and Bess. And whoever was watching the safe house security feed. I fumbled the device from my pocket. There was a new text message from an unknown number and as I read the tiny type, my knees almost buckled.

Kiki, I know you're looking for me. You have to stop. NOW.

My hand shook as the world tilted on its axis then slowly began to spin in the opposite direction.

"Mom?" I said out loud, my voice reedy.

It was true. It was *real*. My mother was alive. My *mother* was *alive*. This was why the German had a list of our safe houses. He really was looking for her. But she hadn't been in any of them, so he'd come after me. She was alive. She was actually freaking alive. I texted back quickly, my hands shaking so much that I had to retype the short message five times.

Mom? Where are you???

Almost the second I hit send, the red exclamation point popped up with that evil message: not delivered.

Of course. A blocked number. But she was out there. She was. It had to be her.

I looked up. Oliver was a block and a half away.

"Oliver!" I wailed. "Stop!"

He must have heard the desperation in my voice because he paused. But he never got the chance to turn, because a big, white van screeched to a halt next to him. I'd taken barely half a step when the door slid open and Oliver was yanked inside.

"Oliver!" I screamed.

I threw Sophia onto the road, jumped on, and pushed pavement, but the van peeled out. I took off after it, panic pounding my heart. Who the hell would kidnap Oliver right off the street? And why? These goons were after me, weren't they? But then, Oliver was with me. So he was fair game.

God, how I wished I had gotten more answers out of that bitch in the meat freezer. How many of Picklebreath's "others" were out there? Were we ever going to get half a second to breathe?

I raced down the street—a four-lane thoroughfare with a double yellow line and traffic lights. Even with Sophia under me, the van was getting further and further away. I was about to lose him for good, when the lights turned red as far as the eye could see and the van pulled to a stop. Kidnappers who obeyed the traffic laws? It was my lucky day.

I turned on the speed, caught up to the van, and jumped off my board. It rolled ahead and bumped to a stop at a sewer drain next to the curb.

"Oliver!" I tried the door, but it didn't budge. I pounded on it so hard my fists stung. Oliver shouted, but I couldn't make out the words.

"Let him go!" I screeched. "He has nothing to do with this!"

The light turned green and they were off again. I groaned, grabbed my board, and followed. As I maneuvered Sophia around an ancient manhole cover I memorized the license plate.

Illinois 851 BCG.

Illinois 851 BCG.

Illinois 851 BCG.

My breath was short, and I honestly felt as if my heart

was about to overload. I couldn't keep up this pace much longer. Up ahead, a police car idled in front of a coffee shop. As I rolled closer I could see two men in blue through the plate glass window, sucking on coffee and laughing.

Would they help me? If I got the cops involved, they'd want my ID. And while I had a fake passport on me, I couldn't risk it being entered in some database and possibly alerting the authorities of my whereabouts. Even more importantly, if the police got Oliver, they'd send him right back to South Carolina, to Robin, to that hell. I couldn't let that happen. Anonymity was key. We really were in this together.

I pressed as hard as I could, almost biffing on some roadkill and hopping the larger cracks in the road. At each light, I closed the distance between us, and I nearly got close enough to grab the back fender, but then the van took off and changed lanes, and I lost my advantage. Then the kidnappers hooked a left onto a residential street, and I made it across the main drag seconds before the light turned green. A motorcycle zoomed past me, so close I swore the driver's leather jacket brushed the back of my backpack.

I turned onto the street and didn't see the van anywhere. It must have pulled into a driveway or a garage. I gave myself ten seconds, gasping for breath as I leaned against a wrought iron fence post, then kept moving.

The street was quiet, aside from dance music playing somewhere in the distance, the repetitive thump of the bass keeping time with my pulse. I hopped off Sophia and ducked down the first driveway on foot, thinking it would be better to stay away from the glare of the streetlights. For a second I crouched next to a busted wood fence and strapped Sophia to my backpack, then cut across a backyard with unkempt grass and a stone barbecue pit at its center.

The garages on the street were all detached and sat at the end of long driveways near the back corner of each property. I paused and took out my Beretta. The steel felt cool against my palm, and I prayed no one would give me a reason to use it. But I would if I had to. I would for Oliver.

At the next house, I peeked inside the foggy garage window and saw nothing but piles of boxes.

The dance music was getting louder. The next garage housed a small car covered by a brown tarp. The third was another mess of storage. At the fourth house, I was close enough to the music to hear the laughter and raised voices that went along with it. I had to scale a fence to get to this garage and when I came down on the other side, I nearly slammed my head against a pile of old kegs. The scent of stale beer hung in the air, and there were cigarette butts everywhere. Lovely.

I brushed myself off and righted my backpack. Cars packed the driveway, and the house was entirely lit up. Two girls hung out on the back porch, smoking and sipping from red cups. Over their heads, propped up on the porch roof, were three illuminated letters. BBГ. And at the very edge of the driveway, hanging over onto the sidewalk, was a big, white van.

What the hell?

A chorus of cheers went up inside the house. My eyes narrowed as I shoved my short, sweaty hair behind my ears. Suddenly, I wasn't in such a rush. I pushed the gun into the back waistband of my jeans and made sure my jacket covered it.

Stepping out of the shadows, I cut across the lawn and walked up the steps to the rear porch where the two girls sat. They eyed me as I strode past and opened the back door.

"Ladies," I said.

One of them scoffed, but neither made a move to stop me. Inside, I found myself in a spacious, brightly lit, mostly white kitchen packed with dozens upon dozens of miniskirt-sporting, overly made-up girls with straightened hair. The dance music was deafening. Everyone was drinking, laughing, shrieking. And in the center of it all was my boyfriend, shirtless, leaning his head back while two buxom babes poured alcohol from two bottles directly down his throat.

"Um, Oliver?" I said.

He brought his chin down too fast and spit brown liquid everywhere. A few drops even landed on my cheek.

"Ew!" the girls chorused.

Oliver wiped the back of his hand across his lips and widened his eyes at me. "They made me do it!"

chapter 13

OLIVER

"WE'RE REALLY SORRY. WE DIDN'T KNOW HE HAD A GIRLFRIEND."

Jessa, the girl with the big boobs and the nasal voice, addressed Kaia, who somehow managed to look threatening, even though the sorority girl had a good six inches on her.

"Our pledge scavenger hunt said 'Blond Hottie,' so…"

She shrugged. I watched Kaia, feeling more than a little bit stupid with alcohol dripping down my bare chest. I'd asked around for my shirt and jacket, but no one seemed to know what had happened to them.

"Uh-huh," Kaia said skeptically. "Do you think you could find his shirt? He looks a little cold, no?"

Jessa scanned me up and down and pressed her tongue into one cheek, smiling in a way that made me feel like I was about to be dragged to her room. Instead, she shrugged again.

"Sure. You guys are welcome to stay and party. There's plenty of food and beer."

She swung around, hair rippling, and dove into the crowd. "This is your pledge class president talking, bitches! If you have the hottie's clothes, you'd better fork them over or I'm gonna dock you points!"

Groans rose up from the crowd. Half a second later, Jessa came back with my shirt, which smelled of strawberries when I pulled it on.

"Have fun!" She twiddled her fingers and was gone.

Kaia snatched my jacket from over the arm of another girl who was sauntering by and tossed it at me.

"I'm really sorry," I said instantly.

"It's not your fault you were kidnapped," Kaia said.

"No. Not for that. I'm sorry about before. For freaking out." I reached for her hand and she let me hold it. "I should have told you what was going on. I just felt so…stupid. I know that's lame, but…I didn't want you to think of me as, like, a victim or something."

"Oliver, it's okay." For the first time since she'd arrived, Kaia's posture softened. "I'm not mad. I wish I'd known. I would have figured out a way to—"

"What? Protect me?" I laughed bitterly. "No one can protect me. All I have to do is make it through my eighteenth birthday in one piece and then I'm outta there."

Kaia leaned forward, pressing her forehead into my chest. "I hate the thought of anyone hurting you."

My heart swelled, and I put my arms around her, backpack and all, resting my chin on top of her head. "I'm okay. And hey… I think we just survived our first fight."

Kaia looked up at me and smiled. "Yeah, I guess we did."

She rose to her toes to kiss me but then pulled away. "Oliver, I have something to tell you."

I raised my eyebrows at her expectantly.

"My mom. She *is* alive."

Kaia showed me her phone, and I read the text. "How do you—"

"My mother is the only person who has ever called me Kiki. It's *her* at the other end of that video feed. She saw my number, and she texted me."

"Oh my God," I whispered.

"I know. I don't have a clue where she is or where she's been, but she's out there."

"Wow." I was happy for her, but at the same time a crater opened in my chest. Kaia's mom was alive. She still had a family. She had people to go home to. People who loved her. And I felt envious. And scared.

Because if Kaia went home to her mother, then where did that leave me? Kaia was all I had. She was my family, and for the last year, I had been hers. But if her real family came back into the picture…

"You guys want?"

A girl with black hair down to her butt held out two paper plates, each with a juicy-looking burger and chips on it. I raised an eyebrow at Kaia.

"Did you not hear what I just said?" she asked.

"Yeah! Yes, I heard you, I swear." I took the two plates and thanked the girl, who walked away to deliver food elsewhere.

"But I also know that we've been on the run for two days, and somehow found ourselves at an actual party where people are having actual fun, and I am starving."

Kaia cast a thoughtful look at the plates. Neither one of us had eaten since our barbecue feast, and that had been at least seven hours and two states ago.

"Wherever your mom is, she's not going to be any more or less findable in the next half hour," I said, slinging my free arm around her shoulders and balancing the plates in my other hand. "I say we stay here for a bit with these lovely Beta Beta Gammas"—a few girls cheered nearby, simply because I'd said their letters—"and relax. For a little while. Come on, Kaia. We're on a road trip. Let's do something, I don't know…fun?"

Kaia tilted her head, considering. "Why do I feel like if we were at a frat house you wouldn't be quite so psyched to stay?"

"Because I am a male person with eyes?" I suggested.

She cracked a smile, then took one of the plates and walked into the living room at the front of the house. All the furniture had been shoved against the walls to make space for a dance floor, so she continued through to the wide front porch. There were a few girls dancing out there, and some guys too, but the porch swing was free. Kaia grabbed it, and I sat next to her.

"We'll stay," she said. "But only if you keep those eyes on me."

I grinned and kissed the corner of her mouth. "Not a problem."

Kaia quickly slipped her gun out of her waistband and

stashed it back in her backpack. I tensed and glanced around, but no one had noticed.

"Good?" I asked as she sat forward again.

She swung her legs under the seat like a little girl.

"Good," she said.

I lifted my burger, but before I took a bite, I held it out to her. I was feeling traitorous over my jealousy and insecurity and wanted to do something about it.

"To finding your mom," I said.

She touched her burger to mine and smiled. "To finding my mom."

chapter 14

KAIA

I LEANED MY HEAD ON OLIVER'S SHOULDER AS WE LOOKED OUT across the Chicago skyline. The Beta Beta Gammas had a rooftop deck with some pretty sick views. On any other night I would have been totally wrapped up in Oliver, enjoying this stolen moment, the two of us free and alone.

But everything was different now. My mother was alive. And all I could do was hope that Oliver hadn't noticed how very elsewhere my mind was. Because the initial elation of knowing she was alive had settled, and slowly, the feeling had been replaced by something else—something that felt a lot less pleasant.

Anger. Betrayal. Confusion.

So maybe three somethings.

Where the hell was she? Why had she left me? How could she go a whole year without contacting me? What was she doing watching security feed of the safe house? Did she know what had happened to my dad?

Whatever the answers to these questions, one thing was abundantly clear. My mother, one of the two people I trusted more than anyone else in the world, had abandoned me. She'd left me behind. Left me for dead. And now she didn't want to be found?

Well screw that. Because now, more than ever, I needed answers. And she was the only person who could give them to me.

I would be back in that Honda right now, gunning it toward who-the-hell-knew-where and coming up with a plan later if it wasn't for how hopeful Oliver had looked when he'd asked me to stay. After his confession on the street earlier, I would have done anything to see him smile. And if that meant hanging out with the girls of Beta Beta Gamma for an hour or two, so be it.

But I can't say I wasn't happy when he brought me up to the roof to be alone.

"How can there be so many people out there that they fill up a city like that?" Oliver mused, kissing the top of my head.

"And every other city on the planet," I replied.

"Can I ask you something?"

A simple question that caused a thump of foreboding in my chest. "Sure."

"Before, when you were asking me who I was…?"

I blushed.

"Who did you *think* I was, exactly?"

Heat crawled up from under my collar and along my jaw line. "I don't really know. FBI, maybe? Homeland Security?"

I wasn't about to tell him that it had crossed my mind that he was a villain. Or a manny.

Oliver guffawed. "No way."

"You do look very sophisticated in my father's clothes," I told him, tweaking his collar.

"I'm flattered, I guess." Oliver shook his head incredulously and slid his arm around me. When he started to laugh, I felt it in my ribs. "Seriously? Me. A government agent."

"All right, all right. I admit it was far-fetched, but cut me some slack. It's been a weird couple of days," I said, straightening out my legs. Down below, the crowd cheered and whooped, probably for another in a long line of keg stands. "But I'm glad you told me the truth. And I'm glad you're out here with me and not back in Charleston with…them."

I looped my arm around his and pulled him closer. I was never going to leave him again. Not ever.

"Me, too." He shifted his weight and pulled something out of his back pocket. Money. "I wanted to give this back to you," he said, averting his eyes.

My whole body tensed. The cash I'd left in the car so he would leave. God, what an asshole I was. "No. You should keep it."

"Kaia," he said. "That's a lot of money."

"I know, but what if we get separated again? Or what if I get hurt?" I said. "You might need it in case I…in case something—"

"We're not gonna get separated again." He pressed the money into my hand. "I promise."

He seemed almost relieved when I took it. I wondered if he'd still sound that sure if he knew how he'd come by that money in the first place. I shoved the cash into the outside pocket on my backpack.

"We need a plan." He clapped his hands and rubbed the together. "Operation Find Kaia's Mom."

My heart skipped about a zillion beats. "My mom," I breathed.

"Maybe she'll know why all these random people are after you, and why they're stalking your safe houses. And, you know, why we got shot at on a Friday afternoon."

"She might even be able to protect us."

"So…any idea where to start?" Oliver asked.

"Not a clue. She could be anywhere. Mexico is the most likely place, since that's where I…where she was taken from."

I looked down at my knees and extricated my arm from his, pressing my sweaty palms into my jeans.

"I wish she'd given me some kind of clue in that text."

"The only thing she *did* say is not to come after her," Oliver pointed out gently. "Are you sure you don't want to listen to her?"

"Listen to the woman who's let me think I was an orphan for the past year?" I scoffed. "Not likely."

"Good point." Oliver sighed. "It's too bad I'm *not* Homeland Security. Then I would know some tech geek who could trace the GPS of the phone the message came from and triangulate your mother's location or whatever. This is what I get for hanging out with doofs like Brian and Hunter. Not a brain cell to spare there."

My entire body went cold. *Triangulate her location.* Why hadn't I thought of that? I knew the answer almost before my mind had formed the question: I'd been too busy wondering why Mom would bail to really concentrate on how to find her. I scrambled to my feet, dragging my backpack with me.

I yanked the photo from my back pocket and stared at the smiling faces of my family.

"Oliver! You're brilliant!"

"I am?" he asked.

I offered him my hand and pulled him to his feet. "Let's get out of here."

"Where're we going?" Oliver asked, following me toward the steps.

I flashed him the photo over my shoulder. "We are going home."

18 MONTHS AGO

THERE WERE FOOTSTEPS ON THE WALK OUTSIDE, CRUNCHING THROUGH gravel and broken glass. My mother's skin looked gray. I shoved my hands under her arms and started dragging her toward the end of the bed.

My mother took a sharp breath. "Kaia, you have to go hide. You have to get out of here."

"Not without you," I said, gasping for breath.

She was so much heavier than she looked.

The footsteps outside slowed. My mother reached up and grasped at my shoulder, then gripped the front of my T-shirt in her fist.

"Kiki, you know the plan, right? You know what to do?"

My chest constricted. "Mom, no. Don't say that. We're getting out of here together."

The footsteps stopped. The doorknob jiggled. With a throat-tearing scream of pain and fear and effort, I pushed us both up off the floor.

chapter 15
OLIVER

"HOME" APPARENTLY MEANT HOUSTON, TEXAS, WHICH WAS A VERY good thing. Because if she'd meant we were going back to South Carolina, I wasn't sure what I'd do. I mean, I would have gone. I would have done anything for her. But I wouldn't have been too psyched about it. The longer I was away from Robin and Jack and that whole mess, the more sure I was that going back was not an option.

Trevor was going to be all right. I had to keep telling myself that until I believed it. And as for college… I'd figure something out. At least now I was safe. Sort of.

Crazy how I could feel safer on the run from unknown assassins than I did in my own home.

But I was so much lighter now that Kaia knew my secret. It was as if I had thousands of weightless bubbles fizzling beneath my skin. Giving her back her money had helped too. I'd felt conspicuous, walking around with all that cash. As if everyone knew what was in my pocket and were scheming to jump me for it. That's what I thought was happening when the sorority chicks grabbed me. I'd thought I was being mugged.

The good news was, there were no more secrets between Kaia and me, and the freedom of that was incredible. It was like I could do anything, be anyone, go anywhere.

It even made the driving a little easier.

Instead of heading southeast toward the Carolinas, we were heading due south, straight through Illinois, and I was back behind the wheel. It was the middle of the night, and there were hardly any cars on the road, so the chances of me doing any real damage were slim to none. We were closing in on Missouri, Kaia sleeping peacefully in the seat next to me, when a pair of headlights flashed in the back window, so close I was blinded. I threw my arm up to block the light from the rearview mirror and the car slammed into our back bumper.

"What the hell?" Kaia blurted, startling awake.

The whole car shimmied.

"That guy came out of nowhere!" I shouted.

I gripped the wheel with both hands and jammed on the brakes.

"No don't! Don't slow down! Floor it!"

"What?" I screeched.

"Do it!"

I pressed the gas pedal toward the floor. All I could see was light. How could she have ever thought I was some kind of super spy? I could barely even keep us on the road.

Kaia rolled down her window and looked out, the wind whipping her hair into her face.

"What're you—"

"There're two guys in the car!" she shouted, sliding back against her seat.

"Is it Scarface?"

"I don't know."

I pushed my foot down on the gas even harder, sweat already pouring from my temples. Kaia fumbled in her backpack. I saw the barrel of the gun glint as she yanked it free.

"What're you gonna do with that?" I blurted.

"What do you think?"

Kaia turned as if to aim out the window. Glowing mile marker signs flew by the car as the lights faded behind us. Maybe I was losing them. Maybe we were going to be okay and she wouldn't have to—

The car behind me suddenly swerved and gunned it. It was coming up on my left side. They pulled up right beside me. Sitting in the passenger seat was a scrawny but vicious-looking guy with dyed orange hair like a Muppet.

"It's not them!" I shouted to Kaia through my terror.

Muppet man shot me an evil smile and then their car slammed into ours.

"What the hell?"

I tried to straighten out the car, but they kept pressing. They were pushing us off the road.

"Oliver!" Kaia screamed, bracing her hand with the gun against her door and grabbing my shoulder with the other.

There was no guardrail between us and whatever lay beyond the highway. My hands yanked on the wheel as if it could do anything to help us, and suddenly, we were airborne.

When I woke up, I tasted blood, and Kaia was crawling over me, shoving open the driver's side door.

"Oliver! Wake up!"

She fell out onto the ground, hands first, and quickly righted herself. Nearby, I heard a door slam. Kaia reached over me and undid my seat belt.

"Come on!" she shouted in my face, gripping my shoulders. "We have to run!"

I felt as if my brains had been knocked loose by the impact, but somehow, I managed to get out of the car. We were at the bottom of an embankment that was covered in brown weeds. Kaia dragged me out of the car and around front. The bumper was gone, the grill dented, the hood flattened like a pancake. Above, there was a flash of light, and I saw someone skidding down the hill.

"Let's go!"

Kaia pulled me into the shoulder high reeds that surrounded the car. I did my best to follow. My vision was shaky, which couldn't be good. As Kaia ran ahead of me I felt like I was watching one of those low-budget horror movies filmed on hand-cams. Except this was real. It was actually happening.

"Where're we going?" I asked stupidly.

"There's a construction site up here," she whispered. "Hurry up."

I did my best to keep pace with her, but my mind felt like it was swimming through soup, and my ears were ringing so loudly it hurt. The brush got taller. It whipped at my face, leaving itchy trails across my skin. I looked behind us and saw nothing but the path we'd made through the reeds. We were alone.

"Kaia. I don't think they're following us. I think we're—"

"You see 'em?" someone shouted. It was impossible to tell from where.

"Over here!"

The second voice was so close I almost screamed. Instead, we ran, sprinting straight ahead for all we were worth. I could hear the men behind me, crashing through the reeds, and at every second I was certain a shot would ring out or a hand would grab me. Half a second or ten minutes later, we emerged from the brush and onto a flat stretch of land. There were about twenty yards of open space between us and what looked like miles of metal scaffolding stretching up against the night sky.

"Where are they?" one guy shouted.

"Just keep moving," the other answered.

"Go! Go! Go!" I cried.

We ran at a crouch and had almost reached the front of a cement truck when I saw the first guy emerge from the weeds.

"There they are!" he cried. And his companion quickly followed.

"Hey you! Kids! Wait up! We just wanna talk!" one of them yelled.

Yeah, right.

Kaia tried the door of the truck, but it was locked.

"What do we do?" she asked.

I stared. She was asking me? I could barely see straight. I looked past her at the framework of the building. My mom and I used to visit my dad at his sites sometimes for lunch. I was always totally fascinated by the elevators that seemed to hang from nothing and the way men could carry huge pipes and rods on one shoulder while scaling ladders. And then, there was the garbage chute. More than anything, as a five-year-old, I had always wanted to slide down a garbage chute.

I grabbed Kaia's hand. "I have an idea."

This time, I took the lead. We ran over to the scaffolding. In the distance I saw a security light blazing from the corner of the foreman's trailer. There was probably a guard in there. Someone who wouldn't appreciate a couple of kids climbing all over the place. All I could do was hope that either (a) he was asleep or (b) he'd read the situation correctly and call the cops. The sight of flashing lights would probably send these guys running.

Actually...

"Call 911," I told Kaia as we reached a set of metal stairs.

"What? I don't even know where we are."

I started to climb and tried to focus, but my vision was still screwy. "The job number. It's on the placard nailed to the trailer. Give them that. Tell them...I don't know...Tell them something."

Kaia dialed as we climbed. There was a turn in the steps every ten stairs and every time we took one, I felt more and more dizzy. I could hear Kaia talking, but I couldn't for the life of me make out her words. At the fourth floor, I had to stop.

"Are you okay?" Kaia asked, breathless.

"Not really." A wave of nausea crashed through me. I gasped in breath after breath. "I think I have a concussion."

I'd had them before. The worst one was during the semi-final game last year against Ridgefield. The world had spun for two straight days. It was the one time in my life Robin had taken real care of me, making sure I didn't watch TV or play video games and that I rested and ate. But that was probably because my social worker was checking in once a day, like actually showing up on the doorstep, during my recovery.

"Shit," Kaia said. "You shouldn't be running around."

I put my head between my knees and took a few deep breaths, hoping it would help. It didn't. "Not like I have much choice."

"Hey blondie! You dyed your hair, huh?!"

We both froze. The voice seemed to echo from everywhere. There was no telling where the guy was. Or his friend.

"Bad move, climbing up there," he shouted. "Lotsa places your dispensable boyfriend can fall from."

The nausea rose to my chest. So nice to know I was dispensable. How the hell had I ended up here? When I'd woken up on Friday morning, I'd thought it was going to be a normal weekend, and now I was climbing scaffolding, and some dude was out to murder me. I mean yeah, Jack could have done that a million times over by now, but he'd never shown up at the house with the goal of putting me in the ground.

At least, I didn't think he had.

"Why, exactly, are we climbing?" Kaia whispered.

"Trust me," I replied. "Keep going."

She shook her head, but she went anyway. I climbed after her, closing my eyes whenever the world got too wobbly, which just made the dizziness worse. Near the seventh floor, we heard the stairs clang. Someone was running after us.

"Get off here," I told her.

"Whatever you say." She sounded dubious.

We turned the corner, and Kaia stopped. I almost ran right into her.

"What?" I asked.

"It's all beams and plywood."

"It's okay," I told her. "The workers walk across these all the time and they weigh twice as much as you do. You see the yellow chute on the other side of the building?"

"Yeah."

"You want to get as close to that as possible."

There was a pause. "You can't be serious."

"As a concussion," I joked, squeezing my eyes closed. When I opened them again she was even more out of focus than before.

"Hold my hand," she said, reaching back for me.

"Oh, honey, are you afraid of heights?" I joked, as my temples throbbed with pain.

"No, *honey,*" she said sarcastically. "I'm afraid that you'll take one wrong step and plunge to your death."

"Oh." My throat went dry. "Good point."

We started across one of the plank walkways. It bowed just a touch, but not too bad. When we got to the center of the floor, Kaia stopped.

"What now?"

"Listen."

The stairs were still clanging. "What?" I said again.

"Only one set of footsteps. Where's the other guy?"

"I don't know," I said. "But I like our odds better now."

Kaia kept moving. I followed her as closely as I could. We were nearing the far side of the building when a shot rang out.

My next footfall hit the edge of a plank, my shoe scraped down, and my fingers slipped from Kaia's. Suddenly I was falling.

"Oliver!" Kaia screamed.

My face collided with the wood plank and my arms instinctively clung to its sides, the edges cutting painfully into the skin inside my elbows. My left leg dangled free while my right was splayed out across the walkway. I could hear someone running. Kaia lunged for me, but before she could touch my shoulder, a gun was trained at my ear.

"I got 'em!" the man shouted. I had no idea whether it was Muppet Man or not. "Freddy! I got 'em!"

Every bone in my body ached, and my lungs were gripped with fear.

"Good!" the other guy shouted back. "Then bring them the hell down here and let's go!"

"What're you gonna do?" Kaia asked.

"Well first, I'm gonna blow this kid's brains out, and then, I'm taking you with me."

A click sounded in my ear. Every muscle in my body tightened. I saw my mom in her hospital bed smiling at me through tears. I saw Trevor cheer the first time he scored a goal while we played soccer in the backyard. I saw my dad on Christmas morning, presenting me with a red bike. And I saw Kaia. A million different memories of Kaia.

I don't want to die! my brain shouted. *I don't want to die I don't want to die I don't want to die.*

"No!" Kaia screamed.

She moved. I felt it more than saw it. Heard the plywood creak.

"What the fuck're you doing?" the man demanded.

I opened my eyes. Kaia had climbed up onto one of the beams at the edge of the building. Her heels dangled over the edge.

"Kaia, no!"

"You hurt him and I jump."

"What?" Me and the guy both asked at the same time. My heart slammed in my chest.

Get down, I thought, staring at Kaia as if she could read my mind. *Get the fuck down.*

"I'm serious. I have no parents. I have no grandparents. He's my family. You kill him, and I have no reason to live," Kaia said. "So put the gun away or I go splat."

She was bluffing, right? She had to be bluffing. I swallowed. I was definitely going to throw up.

"Rico!" the guy shouted from below. "What's going on?"

"We got a situation!" Rico shouted back.

"What kinda situation?"

"Shut up and let me think!"

Kaia looked over her shoulder. I could only hope she'd spotted cop cars in the distance. But part of the plan was to get out of here before they showed. Because if they caught us, they'd send me home. And God only knew what they'd do with Kaia.

"Put the gun away, Rico," Kaia said. "Let him live, and I'll come with you. Otherwise, whatever big-ass payday you've been offered is gone."

"What if I don't believe you?" Rico asked.

Kaia lifted one foot and let it dangle. I tasted bile.

"No!" Rico shouted.

"Kaia," I bit out.

"I'll do it!" she shouted angrily. "I swear I'll do it."

"Stop!" Rico put his hands up, then slowly slipped his gun into the back of his jeans. "There. I put it away." He even took a step away from me. Which was when I remembered the precarious position I was in, gravity-wise.

"Good. Now help him up," Kaia ordered.

Rico clucked his tongue, but reached down and gripped my shirt, hauling me up so I could get on my knees. Shakily, I staggered to the nearest metal post, which I bear hugged with absolutely no shame. Kaia jumped down and ran over to me. She gripped me with only one arm. Rico slowly walked up behind her.

"You okay?" she asked.

"Yeah…you?"

She pulled back and looked me in the eye. Under her breath, she said, "Don't. Move."

What? What was she gonna do now?

"All right, blondie. Let's go."

Rico's hand came down on Kaia's shoulder. She whipped around. I heard a *thunk* and then Rico hit the floor, screaming like an air raid siren.

"What the—"

I looked past Kaia. The handle of her knife stuck out of Rico's thigh.

"Rico! What is it?" Freddy shouted from the ground. "What's wrong?"

Rico kept screaming.

"I'm coming up!"

Kaia yanked the gun out of the waistband of her jeans and pulled back on the top part, training it on Rico. Here she was, getting ready to defend us to the death, and I didn't even know the correct name for that part of the gun.

The wind whipped around us, and I gripped the column tighter.

"You stabbed me!" Rico shouted, finally able to make a coherent sentence. Spittle clung to the corners of his lips. He sounded betrayed. This from the dude who, mere seconds ago, had a gun to my head.

"Who're you working for?" Kaia demanded. "The Iranians? The Malaysians? The Koreans? Who?"

Her arms were steady holding the gun, and I couldn't believe how in control she was.

"Screw you, bitch!" the man spat out.

Kaia lifted her foot and brought it down on the side of the man's injured thigh. He screamed as tears burst from his eyes.

"Is that really necessary?" I asked.

"He was going to kill you, Oliver!" Her look of condescension shocked me. "It was either you or him. At least *he's* still alive."

I could hear Freddy barreling up the stairs. "Okay. Okay," I said, in what I hoped was a soothing voice. "We should probably—"

"Oliver, search his pockets," Kaia said.

"What?"

"ID. I want to know where this jackass is from."

I somehow detached myself from the pillar, but was immediately hit by a wave of nausea so intense, I swear I could taste my stomach lining. I hit my knees, took half a second to breathe, and crawled toward the guy. The first thing my fingers closed around inside his jacket pocket was a used tissue. Awesome. Now I was going to get hepatitis on top of everything else. I yanked his jacket out from under him and found his wallet. Inside was a driver's license.

"Oaxaca." It was the only word I could get out. I tossed the wallet on the wood plank and breathed slowly, in through my nose, out through my mouth, until my stomach went back to its rightful place.

Kaia's jaw clenched. "Who are you working for?" she demanded, pressing her foot down even harder on his leg.

"This guy named Hector hired us, all right? Hector T.!" He let out a wheezing whimper with each labored breath.

"What's the T stand for?"

"I don't know!" the man shouted. "I swear to baby Jesus, I don't know."

"Where's my mother?" Kaia demanded.

"Your mother?"

"You're from Oaxaca!" Kaia replied, her eyes shining. "That's where they took her. You know something! I know you do. What aren't you telling me?"

"Look, I don't know what the hell you're talking about. All I know is this Hector guy has a jones on for you. He hired at least a dozen guys to come after you. I'm just the lucky bastard who got to you first."

Kaia lifted her boot from his leg and he curled into a ball. She looked at me, then lowered her weapon. I cleared my throat and carefully sat back on my butt.

"The name Hector T. mean anything to you?" I asked.

She shook her head. "Nope."

Then she turned, and wretched over the side of the walkway.

Freddy's footsteps were getting closer. I slowly pushed myself up.

"Kaia. It's time to go."

I took her hand and she let me lead her, inching ever so carefully, toward the garbage chute. I glanced inside. I could see maybe three feet before it made its first turn.

"That thing's gonna hold us?" Kaia asked.

"They throw concrete and stuff down here all the time," I said. There was a whoop of sirens in the distance. "We really gotta go."

"You first," she said.

I had zero problem with that. At least if there was something sharp in the Dumpster at the bottom, I would be the one impaled by it. Across the expanse of walkways and beams, the second man emerged onto the seventh floor, heaving for breath. As he reached back for his gun, the plan changed. I shoved Kaia into the tube one moment before the shot shook my eardrums.

Rico moaned, Kaia screamed, and I jumped right down the garbage chute behind her.

chapter 16

KAIA

"Now *this* is how I like to travel."

Oliver dropped into his seat on the Amtrak train at Gateway Station in St. Louis and stretched out his long legs. There was a nasty purple contusion on his cheekbone, and his hair was matted with sweat, but we'd managed to wash all the dirt and grime off our hands and faces in one of the train station's bathrooms. We were covered with cuts and bruises, but at least they were clean cuts and bruises.

Still, a mom passing by our seats veered her kid to the other side of the aisle, putting her body between him and us. I remembered my mom doing that for me, protecting me from the world, the weight of her strong hand on my shoulder, and it made my body ache.

Mom.

I remembered her pressing the gun into my hand that day. The way it slipped in my sweaty palms. I hadn't shot another gun since. But today, I almost had. I'd wanted to.

That man had held his Glock to Oliver's head. And once I had him wrestled to the ground, I'd wanted to kill him more than I'd ever wanted anything. And that scared the crap out of me. Because I'd thought I would never shoot a gun again. I definitely didn't think I'd ever *want* to.

I'd practiced sparring with Henry and Bess and kept up my fitness, but the one time Henry tried to take me to the shooting range I'd had a panic attack. I'd apparently stopped breathing for so long that Bess had freaked out and slapped me across the face to snap me out of it. I'd scared the otherwise unflappable Henry so much, he'd never brought it up again. Now, my arm shook, and I quickly hugged it to my stomach so Oliver wouldn't see the tremor.

"Not that I've ever traveled before," he said cheerfully. "But, you know."

I sat down next to him. "How are you? How's your head?"

"Fine and dandy thanks to that last Red Bull. Between that and all the Excedrin, I've got more caffeine in me right now than your local Starbucks."

After leaving our latest pursuers to be found by the cops, we'd doubled back and borrowed their car. Ours was totaled. Theirs wasn't much better off, but at least it was driveable. It turns out one of the benefits of dating a car expert is that he knows how to start an engine without keys. We drove straight to St. Louis and ditched the ride in the most remote parking space we could find. Then we'd hoofed it to the local drug store to stock up on caffeine, painkillers, and water in case

Oliver really did have a concussion. He'd need to stay awake as long as possible.

Now that we were on the train, I felt slightly more secure than I had on the road. What were the chances that one of our trackers was on this train? They'd have to be clairvoyant. We'd already shoved Sophia and the duffel bags up into the overhead compartments, safe and secure. I tucked my backpack under my feet and leaned my head against Oliver's shoulder.

"Well, *this* is definitely an added benefit," I said, getting comfortable.

I tilted my head and he leaned down to kiss me. It was brief, but it was sweet. After two straight days on the road, I couldn't help wondering how I looked, and even worse, how I smelled. But hopefully, in about sixteen hours, we'd be in Texas, where I could take the longest shower ever recorded by mankind.

If my house was even still there. If it hadn't been sold or repossessed or bulldozed to make way for a new Target. If, if, if.

"Also, I like the fact that no one can run us off the road," Oliver said as the train began to pull away from the station.

"Really? Because I was starting to think the thrill of the chase was kind of...thrilling."

Oliver rolled his eyes and slung his arm around me. I cuddled into his side, an overwhelming wave of gratitude crashing over me. We'd been through a lot in the past two days, but he was still here. He was still by my side. And he, somehow, did not smell bad at all.

"How are *you* doing?" Oliver asked.

"Better now."

"No, I mean…seriously." He nudged my chin up with one finger so I had to look him in the eye. "You weren't really going to jump, were you? I mean…if he'd…you know." Oliver paused and his Adam's apple bobbed. "You wouldn't have actually killed yourself."

I took a breath. "I don't know."

It was the honest truth. If Oliver had died, if I'd seen his brains get splattered all over the plywood, I wasn't sure I wouldn't have taken that step.

Oliver was silent. "Thank you for saving me," he said eventually.

My lips twitched. "Anytime."

He kissed my head again and toyed with my fingers in my lap. "That was pretty gruesome, though. With the knife."

My stomach shifted, as if it couldn't get comfortable inside my body. "Yeah."

"I don't know how you did it. I don't think I could ever shove a knife into another person."

"I did it to save us," I snapped.

"I know," Oliver said.

"I don't think you do," I said. "You keep making these judgey comments… It's like you think I enjoy violence or something."

I was vibrating, suddenly, as a memory came back to

me, full force. I saw the boy in my head. Saw him stare at me, confused—almost betrayed. I saw him fall.

"I don't think that," Oliver said quietly.

"Well, good. Because I don't, okay? I'm only doing what I have to do to keep us alive. And to figure out our next move."

Oliver raised his hands in surrender as best he could with one arm behind me. "Okay," he said. "I understand."

I took a deep breath and blew it out. "Good."

Oliver studied me, and for a second I thought he was going to press the issue, but then, he kissed my forehead. "Good."

We sat in silence for a few minutes, and I tried to relax. I knew from experience that once that kid's face entered my mind, it was near impossible to get rid of, so I concentrated as hard as I could on my breathing. On Oliver's breathing.

"So, speaking of next moves, who is this Hector T. person?" Oliver asked.

"I don't know." My foot bounced beneath me. I hadn't ingested any of Oliver's caffeine stash, but I felt like I had. I was so wired my heart was floundering. "Clearly he's yet another person my parents pissed off."

I sat up a little to slide the old photograph of me and my parents out of my back pocket and held it in my lap so the both of us could see. "It used to be I didn't want them to tell me what they were doing. I didn't want to imagine them doing it, you know?"

I glanced up at him, and he ran his hand through the tangled mess of my hair. I'd had a fight with my parents a couple of weeks before Oaxaca. I'd told them I couldn't take our life anymore. The constant worrying. Never knowing if they were coming back to whatever hotel we were calling home. I'd told them I wanted to stay in Houston, enroll at a normal school, have a normal life.

"It's not possible," my mother had said. "*This* is our life."

"I hate our life," I'd shouted at the two of them. "I hate you."

The hurt had been plain in my father's tired blue eyes. Even then, there had been a bruise on his right cheek—purple and yellow and blue. "You don't mean that, Kaia," he'd said.

"Yes, I do," I'd countered. "I'd give anything for normal parents. But you two will never be normal. I can't wait until I'm eighteen so I can get away from you!"

And then I'd done the most childish thing imaginable. I'd stormed up to my room and slammed the door. I could still hear the slam in the back of my mind. Sometimes it sounded like a gunshot.

"I get that," Oliver assured me.

"But now...now I wish I knew more," I told him, staring at my father's laughing face in the photo. "Maybe then I'd know where to look for her. Maybe then I'd know who Hector T. was and why he, and all these other people, are after me."

"Do you think Scarface is Hector T.? He kinda looked like a Hector T."

I shivered at the memory of Scarface describing me to the man behind the gas station convenience store's counter. I didn't want to think about him or what he might have done to my mother that day more than a year ago. I looked into Mom's eyes in the photo and bit back my sorrow. If I'd been stronger, quicker, more in control—if my mother hadn't had to protect me—would any of this have happened? Would my family still be together?

"I don't know," I said again. "Maybe Scarface is Hector."

But if my family were still together, I never would have met Oliver. *We* wouldn't be together right now.

"Do you think he hired that woman in Kentucky too?"

I lifted my shoulders. Now both my feet were bouncing. I chewed on my bottom lip. "Maybe, but I don't know. India Air… It doesn't seem like I was supposed to be flying to Oaxaca."

I didn't want to think about Hector T. anymore. Or bounty hunters. Or Scarface. I didn't want to think about anything. But I couldn't stop myself. It was like I was thinking about everything all at once, and none of it made sense.

"We're going to be okay," Oliver whispered. "We'll figure it out. Why don't you try to get some sleep?"

"I can't. I need to help you stay up."

"Oh, believe me. I'm staying up."

His pupils were so tiny I didn't dare dispute him. I looked down at the photo, still clutched between my thumbs and forefingers.

"I don't think I can," I admitted. "There's too much going on in my head."

"C'mere."

Oliver shifted so that I was mostly laying down, my side splayed across the double seat. In this position, I could clearly hear his heart beat, and it was pounding hard and fast. I breathed in and out, listening to its rhythm. Oliver ran his hand over my hair gently, and I felt my eyelids go heavy.

"Did I ever tell you about the time my mom took me to visit her grandfather at his farm?"

He had, but I didn't care. I loved this story. I loved listening to his voice. He was working his magic.

"Mmmmhmmm," I murmured.

"I was five years old, and the only thing I wanted was my very own pig," he began, his voice a low rumble in his chest. "So my mother took me out to the farm to pick one out, but when we got there, there were no pigs. Just puppies."

I smiled, the train rocking us back and forth. My eyelids fluttered closed.

"Turned out, my mom had another pet in mind…"

The last thing I felt before I passed out was Oliver's warm, lingering kiss on my forehead.

The ropes were tight against my skin. So tight I couldn't move my hands even a millimeter. My shoulder muscles ached from the strain of my wrists being bound so firmly behind me. I was scared. My teeth chattered, and snot ran down over my lips.

A man paced in the shadows. I couldn't see his face, only

the occasional glint of the knife as it caught the glow of a stray moonbeam.

"Please don't hurt us. Please. Please!"

In the corner, something moved, shifting weight, making the floors groan.

The man stepped out of the shadows. His scar shone a purply red in the moonlight, the skin around its edges glossy. Scarface.

"Please…," I cried. "We just want to go home. Please let us go home."

"Oh, but that would mean you had a home to go to, Kiki." Another man had appeared next to the first. The Handsome Man. The sound of my mother's nickname for me on his tongue almost made me vomit.

Scarface laughed. He brought the knife to my cheek, and I tried to recoil, but I couldn't move. My feet were tied to the legs of the chair. I couldn't move at all. The tip of the blade dug into my skin.

I screamed.

"I'm going to give you a scar," he said, "A scar exactly. Like. Mine."

The Handsome Man sighed and checked his watch as the pain dug deeper and deeper and my scream grew shriller and shriller. The floorboards in the corner groaned again, and my mother stepped into the light. She looked angry. Disappointed. She couldn't even look me in the eye.

"Mom!" I screamed as the blade cut toward my ear. "Do something! Stop him! Stop him, please!"

"You're the only one who can stop this, Kiki," she snapped. *"You have to stop. Now!"*

I woke with a start and glanced around the train car. The sun had gone down, and the only light came from the overhead lamps. Oliver was passed out. My heart lurched at the sight of him with his eyes closed, but then he muttered something under his breath, clearly alive and well. But the dream clung to me.

The Handsome Man. I had almost forgotten what he'd looked like until that dream had brought his image back in detail. I remembered the strange things he'd said to my mother that day. The way he'd focused his dark eyes on her, as if he was seeing a precious jewel for the first time—and he wanted to crack it between his teeth.

I pushed my hair back from my face and took a few calming breaths, trying to soothe my panicked heart. The images from the dream began to fade, but my cheek stung where the German had cut me two days before. The wound felt fresh. I put my feet flat on the floor, and my heart sunk into my toes.

My backpack was not where I had left it.

I leaned forward to see under my seat. It wasn't there. I checked under Oliver's seat, under the seats in front of ours, and then, in a fit of desperation, in the overhead rack. Our duffels were still there. And Sophia. We still had our clothes and some food. But my backpack was gone.

My foot slipped and I saw the edge of my family photo

sticking out from under my boot. I bent to retrieve it, using the side of my sleeve to wipe away the tread marks. At least I hadn't been robbed of the photo.

But the bag that held our money, my iPad, my gun—everything of real value I possessed—was gone.

chapter 17
OLIVER

"I CAN'T BELIEVE HOW HARD THIS SUCKS."

"Will you stop? It's not your fault," Kaia said, turning to walk backward and sticking her thumb in the air, her board tucked under her arm. The driver of the Chevy coming toward us honked his horn but didn't slow down. Kaia waved her hand in front of her face, trying to bat away the dust the car's tires had kicked up.

"I was supposed to stay awake. That was my only job. Instead I crashed, and look what happened!" I adjusted the strap of my duffel on my shoulder. The sleeping bag tied to it bumped my hip as we walked. I was dying from the heat of walking for an hour under the midday Texas sun. To make everything worse, I'd woken up with a mind-bending headache that not even half a bottle of Excedrin could touch, which didn't exactly put me in the best mood. "I should go home. What'm I even doing here?"

"Oliver—"

"No! I'm serious. You'd probably be better off on your own."

I couldn't believe we'd made it this far, that we'd gotten so close to Kaia's home and maybe some answers and, at the very least, a shower, and some random jerk had stolen her bag. All that money. Gone. If only a couple of bills had slipped out of her bag, like they had back at the rest stop. Or if I had kept the thousand in my pocket when she'd told me to. Then at least we'd have enough money for a cab. Why couldn't I have woken up and caught the guy trying to make off with her stuff? Why did I sleep through everything?

"If it's anyone's fault, it's mine." Kaia threw her palm up as another car blew by us. "I was too tired to think. I should've at least wrapped the strap around my leg or something."

"So we both suck. Great. That makes me feel so much better."

I chugged some water, hoping it would take the edge off the pain in the back of my skull. It didn't.

"Could it be any hotter in this godforsaken place?"

Kaia dropped her duffel and skateboard in the dirt on the side of the road, and put her hands on her hips. "What is your deal?"

"My deal?" I asked, annoyed. "What do you mean what's my deal?"

"I mean, I love you, but if you don't shift gears in the next two seconds, I can't be responsible for my actions." An eighteen-wheeler laid on his horn as he drove by, and it was like someone was drilling an ice pick directly into my head. The dust pelted my face like a thousand tiny cannonballs. "I already have enough going on without your cranky pants attitude."

I stared at Kaia, and as irritated and overtired, dirty and emotionally spent and in-pain as I was, a laugh bubbled up in my throat.

"I'm sorry. Did you just call me 'cranky pants'?"

She almost smiled but didn't. "I believe the phrase I used was 'cranky pants attitude.' I called your attitude 'cranky pants.'"

I laughed and Kaia did too. I closed the space between us and wrapped my arms around her tightly, which prompted another tractor-trailer to blare on his horn. Kaia turned her face and rested her cheek against my chest. My headache eased ever so slightly.

"I'm sorry. You're right," I said into her hair. "Whining about the situation doesn't help the situation. Doing something does."

"That's very deep," she told me.

"One of my grief counselors said that to me like six months after my mom died and two months after my dad left."

"He said that to a foster kid who couldn't do anything to help his situation?" Kaia looked at me, appalled. "Sounds like he wasn't very good at his job."

"Yeah, he was pretty much an asshole." I ran my hand over her cheek and kissed her lips. "I wish I'd known you back then."

"When we were eight?" she said. "No you don't. I was in a very antiboys stage at eight and I had a working slingshot. I probably would've nailed you with a rock."

"At least I would've had your attention."

I leaned down and kissed her, and for a moment everything was okay. Except when we parted, we were still stuck on a highway on the west side of Houston, miles away from her house on the east side, and my head was still throbbing. I spotted another strip mall in the distance. Houston seemed to be made up entirely of strip malls. But this one had a garish sign strung across the front of one store. It read: **WE BUY AND SELL USED CELL PHONES!**

And suddenly I had an idea. Maybe, after all this time, I could finally put the asshole's advice to good use.

"Come on." I tugged on Kaia's hand, hoofing it double-time toward the mall.

"Where're we going?"

"I'm going to stop whining and start doing."

It wasn't until we were standing directly under the sign that Kaia figured out my plan.

"I can't sell my phone," she said. "What if my mom texts me again?"

"We're not selling your phone. We're selling mine."

I opened the door to the shop, and the air conditioning blasted out, throwing its arms around me like an old friend. Sweet relief. The pounding in my head dialed down to a dull tap. Kaia grabbed my hand and pulled me back to the sidewalk.

"No, no, no. You can't sell your phone. You worked forever to save enough to buy that thing."

Which was true. My part-time job at the auto parts place paid minimum wage before taxes and Robin took half of my net pay and I still had to buy some things for myself. Like lunch. And pencils. And underwear. My phone was my prized possession. But it no longer mattered. It was part of my past—a past that I had no intention of revisiting.

"Let's see how much my work is worth in Texas."

I tugged out the phone, grinned, and walked into the store. Ten minutes of haggling later, I walked out with a hundred dollars.

"You think this is enough to get a cab back to your place?" I asked Kaia.

She took a deep breath. "Only one way to find out."

chapter 18

KAIA

OLIVER WAS BARTERING WITH THE CAB DRIVER, TRYING TO TIP HIM with cans of soup, when we pulled up in front of my house, and their conversation faded into the background. A lump the size of a soccer ball formed in my throat. The house was exactly the same.

Same olive-green siding, same intricate white trim, same yellow and purple flowers bursting from the flower boxes. My parents' rocking chairs sat on the porch, angled toward each other as if waiting for them to walk out the front door with glasses of lemonade. Next to them was the wicker couch that I'd always laid out on, my knees crooked over the arm, my bare feet dangling down the side closest to my father, so he could tickle them. The door was the same burgundy color and looked freshly painted. The lawn was recently mowed.

Was someone living here?

My heart seized.

Was my *mother* living here?

What if I walked through the door, and she was sitting on the couch in her old, fluffy pink slippers, waiting for me?

What if, all along, all I'd needed to do was come home? The idea made me queasy with excitement and dread.

The taxi's door opened, and Oliver was there, right in front of me. I blinked up at him. I hadn't even heard him get out of the car. He offered his hand, but I ignored it and shoved myself out, feeling silly. I walked to the end of the driveway and looked at the garage. I could see the top of my father's silver SUV through the garage door window. I felt disoriented, as if I'd stepped into a time warp.

"What?" Oliver asked. "What is it?"

"My dad's car. It's still here."

If anyone was living here, it wasn't a new family.

My pulse raced. I bounded up the porch steps and over to the fourth shingle under the second window, jabbing my fingers up under the crease. A key fell into my hand and the lump in my throat widened.

"You okay?" Oliver asked.

All I could do was nod. Tears were threatening to spill over. I shoved the key into the lock, turned it, and pushed open the door, quaking with pent-up emotions—anticipation battling it out with hope and anger and fear.

No one was home. That was obvious the second I stepped inside. The air was stale with the scent of too many hot days with windows locked tight. A thin layer of dust had accumulated on the table next to the stairs, where my mother's favorite framed picture of our family sat. I ran a finger through the dust and swallowed.

Oliver squeezed my shoulders. "So," he said lightly. "This is where you grew up."

"Sort of. I mean, we were hardly ever here, but…we were here more than any other place. My parents called it 'home base.'"

Oliver kissed my cheek and squeezed my shoulders again, grounding me. Reminding me that even though my parents weren't here, he was. He headed toward the foot of the stairs.

"What're you doing?" I asked, swiping a hand across my cheek.

His fingers curled around the top of the newel post and he grinned. "I'm going to go see your room."

Oh crap.

"Oliver! Oliver, no!"

But he'd gotten a lead on me. By the time I made it to the second floor he was already throwing open doors. To the bathroom, the linen closet, the spare room, and then—

"Don't," I said, eyeing his hand on the doorknob.

"Oh, but I have to," he replied playfully.

He opened the door, and a shaft of pink light engulfed him.

"Oh. My. God. It's like a My Little Pony shrine in here!"

My love of pink had come from my mother. But while she had used the color as a mere accent—a bag strap here, a beaded bracelet there, the occasional stripe on a headband—I had embraced the color with every fiber of my being. When I was four.

"You can*not* judge me by this room!" I said, arriving at the door as he flung himself, face up, onto my canopy bed.

Damn. It was even pinker than I remembered. A light pink rug, pink and hot pink striped walls, a pink flowered canopy and pink plaid sheets. There were pink stuffed animals, a pink-framed mirror, pink bookshelves filled with pink and purple and white books and toys and knickknacks. There was no color in the room other than pink and white and purple. Except for Oliver. He was all gray T-shirt and tan skin and blond hair.

"I never had you pegged for a Disney Princess," Oliver said, pushing himself up on his elbows.

I walked over and sat next to him. The bed gave a familiar squeak. "I thought about changing it when I was thirteen, but we never got around to it. We were rarely here, so it didn't seem to matter. I never even thought about the fact that a guy might see it one day."

"Are you saying I'm the first guy you ever invited into your Barbie Dreamhouse?"

"I didn't exactly invite you," I pointed out, shoving his chest. "You barreled right in."

Oliver reached an arm around my waist. He got that look in his eye he only got when we were entirely alone. It made my heart catch.

"Just like the day we met."

I smiled. The day we met. Probably the single best day of my life.

Now, an entire year of kisses and phone calls and texts and adventures and secrets and whispers and near-death experiences between us, we were sitting in my pink explosion of a room, and I was overwhelmed by the sheer luck I felt at finding him. I leaned down and kissed him. He pulled me to him, pressing the whole length of his body against mine, and slid his hand under my short hair, around the back of my neck. We kissed for a long time, legs intertwining, chests bumping, hands exploring. For those few spare minutes, there was only Oliver.

Then he rolled me onto my back, and I winced as one particular bruise on my spine ached. I sat up, remembering why we were here. Oliver almost fell off the bed.

"What? What's wrong?" he said.

"Oliver," I replied, gasping for air. "I have to show you something."

chapter 19

OLIVER

Kᴀɪᴀ ᴘᴀᴜꜱᴇᴅ ꜰᴏʀ ᴀ ᴍᴏᴍᴇɴᴛ ᴏɴ ᴛʜᴇ ᴛʜʀᴇꜱʜᴏʟᴅ ᴛᴏ ʜᴇʀ ᴘᴀʀᴇɴᴛꜱ' room. It was so quick, someone who didn't know her as well as I knew her might not have even noticed. I could only imagine how hard it must be for her to be there without them. I couldn't even remember what my parents' bedroom had looked like before my mom got sick. My only memories of it were lines of orange prescription bottles, the raspy sound of the breathing machine, and my mom's soft skin when she held my hand.

Kaia walked over to the closet. The door creaked as she opened it. She shoved aside a row of men's suits and shirts and disappeared inside.

"Kaia? What're you—"

I stopped when I heard the hum followed by a low click. When I stepped in behind Kaia, she was no longer in the closet. She'd entered a whole new room, and the sight of it made my inner ten-year-old jump up and cheer.

"Whoa."

"Welcome to the Batcave," Kaia said.

The Batcave was a long, shallow room with two utilitarian tables and two leather chairs. Set up on the tables were four impressive flat-screen monitors. Tall towers of black servers covered the wall behind those monitors. There were blinking lights and wires everywhere. As I stepped inside I saw glass-front cases lining another wall, and inside were shelves upon shelves of spy gear. There were goggles, glasses, watches, cameras, helmets, recording devices, pens in velvet cases that must have served some purpose other than writing. Another cabinet held a crossbow, nunchakus, a staff, a few pairs of handcuffs, some handguns, and about a dozen glinting knives.

"This is intense," I said under my breath.

Kaia took a handgun from the weapons case—one that looked exactly like the gun she'd had in her stolen backpack—and laid it on the table, then booted up the computers. The monitors blinked to life, their screens glowing bright green. Each one displayed a box in the center of its screen asking for a password. Kaia typed on one of the keyboards and the monitors turned black.

"We're in," she said.

"Your family is *so* cool," I said.

Kaia went rigid, and I realized that was a pretty dumb thing to say. Her father was most likely dead, and her presumed-dead mom had abandoned her for more than a year and then basically told her to screw off.

But still. At least she'd had a family for sixteen years. At least she had parents who loved her for a while. She could remember how that felt. And this… I'm sorry, but this set up was awesome.

Kaia plugged her phone into one of the computers. "Thank God this was in my pocket and not in my bag," she muttered.

Instantly a program booted up. She sat and typed like crazy, her fingers flying over the keyboard.

"Come on," she said under her breath. Her knee danced its own manic hip-hop routine under the desk. "Come on…"

After a few slams on the return button, she cursed under her breath.

"What's wrong?" I asked. "Can you track your mom?"

She swiveled the chair around and shoved herself away from the seat, the anger pulsating off of her. "Sure. Sure I can track her." She grasped her locket and pulled the chain taut until the skin of her neck turned white around it. "But it's gonna take hours. Maybe even days."

"Kaia, are you—"

"I'm fine, all right?" She paced past me out into the bedroom, her boots leaving footprints in the thick, light gray carpet. "I'm great. My mother wants to play games now? Fine! We'll play her games! We'll play her *fucking* games."

Kaia stormed over to one of the dressers, yanked out the top drawer and upended the contents all over the floor. Underwear and bras fluttered into a pile at her feet. She turned and, with a cry, threw the drawer at the wall. It made a brown dent and thumped to the floor. Then she went for the next one.

"Kaia! Calm down!"

"I am calm! I'm perfectly calm!" Kaia shouted, adding a deluge of socks and tights to the pile of clothing. "Why wouldn't I be calm? My mother, who is back from the dead, has also cloaked her position so that her GPS signal is pinging off of satellites all over the damned universe! My mother, who supposedly loved me, is so intent on hiding from me that she's involved the fucking Russians!"

She yanked out another drawer and it banged to the floor. She tore out neatly folded sweaters and shirts, chucking them over her shoulders.

"She's involved the entire freaking planet! But I'll play along! I'll keep searching for clues! I'm enough of a pathetic loser that I can't take a hint!"

She yanked out another drawer and it fell with a thud, crushing her fingers between it and the one on the floor.

"Ow! Sonofabitch!"

I dropped to my knees next to Kaia as she burst into tears. She stuck her injured fingers in her mouth as her chest heaved. I put an arm around her and gently tugged the fingers from her lips. She turned her cheek to my shoulder and sobbed.

I held onto her for all I was worth and clenched my teeth, wishing I could absorb her pain. I wished I could find her mother and kill her for making Kaia hurt like this. But I couldn't do either of those things, so I let her cry until her tears finally slowed and she took in one snotty, shaky breath.

"I'm sorry," she said, and her voice broke.

"Are you kidding? I'm surprised you didn't crack before this."

I kissed her forehead and ran my hand over her hair. As I shifted position, something over Kaia's shoulder caught my eye. When she'd yanked out the drawers, she'd exposed the floor under the dresser, and tucked under it, against the wall, was a brown shirt box.

"What's that?" I asked.

Kaia turned to look. "I don't know."

She tugged out the box. It was covered in dust. A pink ribbon was tied around it, worn and faded, as if it had been tied and untied a million times.

"Open it," I prodded.

Kaia tugged at the ribbon and it came undone. She tipped the lid, then let it fall back onto the carpet. Inside was a pile of old and yellowed birthday cards; a tiny, clear box full of what looked like sand; a battered rag doll; and a black and white photograph of a little girl on her mother's lap. The mom was laughing at something or someone off screen. The girl was staring up at her mother like she'd never seen anyone so captivating in her life.

Her fingers shaking, Kaia reached for the birthday card on the top of the pile. The message was in Spanish, but I'd studied it long enough to know what it said.

Feliz cumpleaños a mi niña.

Happy Birthday to my little girl.

Kaia opened the card and read, translating for me. "Dearest Marissa. I can't believe you're fourteen years old! Where has the time gone? It seems like yesterday you were strapped to my back in the yard, laughing whenever I bent to pull at a weed. No matter how tall and beautiful you get, Marissa, you will always be my baby girl. I love you forever. Love, Mom."

"Who's Marissa?" I asked.

Kaia slowly put the card down, placed the top back on the box, pushed herself up, and walked out of the room without a word.

18 MONTHS AGO

I CARRIED MY MOTHER AS FAR AS MY ROOM, BUT WHEN WE WERE through the door, my muscles gave out. With a cry of desperate frustration, I sank to the floor, bringing her with me. We managed to crawl to the corner, both of us covered in sweat and tears. I reached over and slammed the adjoining door with my foot. At the exact same moment, the outer door to her room—the one the people after us had been pounding on—shattered.

My mother writhed, pulling her gun from the waistband of her jeans. She pressed it into my hand.

"Mom...what?"

"Whoever comes through that door, shoot him," she said, looking me dead in the eye.

"No way! I can't shoot someone. I've only shot at soda bottles. I don't think I can—"

Someone kicked at the adjoining door, and it shuddered at the force.

"You can and you will." Her eyes seemed to tremble in their sockets. "Never stop fighting, right mija?"

Her head slumped toward my shoulder. "Mom? Mom!?"

There was another kick followed by a splintering sound. The door was about to give. I lifted the gun, holding it with both hands. My arms were shaking so hard they hurt. I could no longer hear my mother breathing.

"Mom?" I whispered. "Mom...please."

The door burst open, and the gun went off.

chapter 20
KAIA

I WOKE UP TO PITCH-BLACKNESS WITH AN AWFUL FEELING OF DREAD in the pit between my heart and my stomach. I'd heard a sound, but I didn't know what. Lying on my stomach, I pushed myself up on my hands. Oliver lay next to me, sleeping like a baby on top of my pink comforter in my dad's striped pajama pants and a clean, white T-shirt. After a few breaths, I decided I was being paranoid. The house was silent. I was about to lie down again, when the floorboards on the stairs creaked.

I silently slipped out of bed and fumbled for my gun before I remembered I'd left it in the Batcave. There was no time to get it. Desperate, I grabbed Sophia off the floor and pressed my back against the wall next to the door.

Another creak. Oliver didn't move. Damn, this kid was a heavy sleeper. The sight of him dozing so peacefully made me feel guilty for the way I'd treated him when I'd stalked out of my parents' bedroom. I'd barely said another word the rest of the night.

Marissa…Marissa…Marissa…

The name burned inside my chest and behind my eyelids every time I closed my eyes. But how could I explain that to Oliver? I couldn't, so I'd basically shut down.

Another creak. I said a silent prayer, my fingers gripping my skateboard for dear life. Half a second later, and I could hear the intruder breathing. He paused at the open doorway to my room, looking in at Oliver. I could see only a hand, the toe of one black boot, the front of a black jacket pulled taut over a sizable belly. Not Scarface, thank God. But could it be his partner? The guy Oliver leveled back in South Carolina? The man took a step toward the bed. I gritted my teeth and brought my skateboard down over his head as hard as I could.

"Oof!"

Oliver startled in bed, bleary-eyed and confused. "What? What?"

The man went down. I lifted my arms to try to hit him again, but his foot darted out and swept both of mine, sending me sprawling onto my ass. Sophia rolled into the hall as my already-bruised back exploded in pain. The man pushed himself to his knees, then his feet, and trained a gun on Oliver.

"No!" I shouted, and side tackled the intruder into my desk, which crumbled on impact.

Oliver dove behind the bed as the gun clattered to the floor and skidded across the hardwood. I dragged the man to his feet by the back of his jacket and flung him across the room. He teetered, spun, arms akimbo, until Oliver laid him out with a right hook to his jaw. The intruder slammed into the bookshelf, knocking ceramic unicorns onto the floor where they bounced and shattered. He slid down, groaning, and came to rest half-propped against the shelving, his legs crooked beneath him.

I hit the switch, turning on the overhead lights. Oliver and I blinked against the sudden brightness. The man groaned again, holding his side, pushing his feet out weakly. My breath caught in my throat. It couldn't be.

"Uncle Marco?"

The man's eyes fluttered open, and he stared at me, looking as if he'd seen a ghost. "Kaia?" He shook his head. "You went blond."

"Yeah, I did." I couldn't believe it. I couldn't believe he was actually here. "And you got fat."

He chuckled, and licked a speck of blood off his lip. "Good to see you, too, kid."

chapter 21

OLIVER

"WHAT'RE YOU DOING HERE?" KAIA ASKED. "I THOUGHT YOU WERE living in Reno."

I came out of the bomb-shelter-style pantry with three cans of chicken noodle soup and a box of saltines and placed them on the kitchen counter. It was after midnight, and outside the kitchen windows it was dark except for the occasional security light over a neighbor's garage door. Kaia was sitting at the kitchen table with her uncle Marco, who I already didn't like. There wasn't any concrete reason. I knew that Kaia had been hoping to find him, but his presence felt like an intrusion. We'd been alone, a team, for the last few days. Me and Kaia against whatever unnameable forces were hunting us. We didn't need anyone else.

Call it childish, but I didn't want him here. And honestly? I wasn't entirely sure Kaia wanted him here either.

She'd seemed happy to see him at first—happier and more at ease than she'd been since we found that memory box in her parents' room—but once he'd been checked over for bruises and breaks, she'd kept her distance. Like now. Her arms were crossed over her chest, and her leg bounced under the table. She'd picked the seat furthest from his and could barely manage to hold eye contact with the guy for more than two seconds.

"Your mom and I had a system. If she didn't call me within a week of when a job was scheduled to be completed, I was supposed to fly here to check on you guys," Marco said. He had a gruff voice. Gravelly. Like he'd swallowed pebbles. His speech had a trace of a Mexican accent that faded in and out. "But you never came back."

I found a pot, dumped in the soup, and put it on the stove on high. Something he'd said was niggling at the back of my brain, but I couldn't put my finger on it. I was both too tired and too wired to concentrate. Part of me wanted to join them at the table to show Marco he didn't intimidate me. But he did. He was Kaia's family. An authority figure. They had a history together. Plus, he'd barely acknowledged my existence when Kaia had introduced me and hadn't said a word to me since. I couldn't make myself bridge the gap and assert my presence, so I hung out at the counter, feeling awkward.

"I been taking care a' the outside a' the house like I promised. Your parents always said if something went sideways, I needed to keep mowing the lawn, fixing up what was broke, all that kinda stuff. Keep up appearances, ya know?"

"Makes sense," Kaia said, reaching up to touch her locket.

Marco sat forward in his seat. His glass eye stared slightly to the left of whatever his good eye was looking at, and it made me feel like he was trying to keep an eye on me.

"I still can't believe it," he said. "I thought you were dead, kid. I thought all three a' ya were gone for good."

He reached across the table for her hand, his leather jacket creaking. She reluctantly gave it to him, but only for a second before refolding her arms.

"I thought we were too," Kaia said.

That's when it hit me. Kaia had told me that she hadn't been with her parents in Oaxaca. She'd told me she'd stayed here with her uncle Marco. But clearly…

I found myself staring at Kaia, my heart in my throat. She avoided my gaze.

Marco sat back in his chair and rubbed his eyes, then grunted a sigh. The soup started to bubble, so I started opening cabinets and drawers to find bowls and spoons and napkins. Honestly, I was grateful I had something to do with my hands. Kaia had lied. Again. She'd been there when her parents went missing. But why? Why would she lie about that?

"So what happened? Where're Elena and David? And what're you doing here with surfer boy?" Marco jabbed a thumb over in my direction. He still didn't bother to look at me.

I gritted my teeth.

"I've never been surfing in my life," I said, and dropped a bowl of soup in front of him with a clatter.

"It's a look, kid." He didn't even turn his head in my direction. "You got the look."

"Actually, I was hoping you could tell me where my parents are," Kaia said flatly as I walked around behind her.

Marco's good eye flashed, alarmed. "Tell you what?"

"Where my mother is."

He was almost too still. His leather jacket, which had been squeaking and cracking the whole time they'd been talking, fell silent. "If you don't know how the hell'm I supposed to know?"

Kaia pulled out her phone and slid it across the table to him, face up. I sat down next to her with our bowls of soup but kept my distance. I felt like if I got too close to her, I'd start spouting questions at her, and now was not the time.

"I got this text a couple of days ago. The computer in the Batcave is trying to trace the GPS," she said.

"You have the code to the Batcave?" Marco asked.

Kaia blinked. "You don't?"

Marco huffed and tugged on the front of his jacket. There was some kind of power play happening between the two of them that I couldn't quite follow.

"Come on, Marco. Are you really going to tell me you don't know where your sister is?"

Marco picked up the phone between thumb and forefinger. It was like he didn't want to touch it. He tilted his head back and held the screen at arm's length to read it.

"Tell me everything that happened."

He leaned over his bowl and started to shovel chicken and noodles past his lips like he hadn't eaten in days. I stared at the side of Kaia's face, wondering if I was finally going to hear the truth.

"Everything?" She glanced at me, and I knew that she knew what I was thinking.

"I can't help ya if I don't know what happened," Marco said.

Kaia took a deep breath. "We were in Oaxaca," she began.

Marco paused. Broth dripped from his spoon. "Oaxaca?"

"So you *were* there," I said.

Kaia nodded. "I was there."

I dropped my spoon into my bowl, appetite quashed.

"We were in Oaxaca, and Dad was out scouting a job," she continued. "They'd been hired to take out some politician."

"Which one?" Marco asked.

"You know they never gave me specifics."

"I also know how good you are at eavesdropping."

Kaia paused. "Fine. Miguel Feliciano." She eyed Marco up and down. "Why?"

"No reason."

Yeah, right. This guy had the worst poker face ever. My gut was telling me something was going on here, something bigger than Kaia's lies, but I had no idea what.

Kaia shifted in her seat. Something had gotten under her skin too.

"Miguel Feliciano's still alive," Marco said, staring at Kaia.

"That would be because my parents never got to finish the job."

Marco cursed under his breath. "Why not? What happened?"

"We were waiting for my dad to get back when Mom got this text from him telling us to run. Two seconds later, the hotel room was shot to high hell."

"You were shot at? Were you hurt?" I asked.

Kaia voice was quiet. "No, but my mom was. She was shot in the leg and the shoulder."

Marco took a breath and rubbed a hand up and down his face. His eyes went watery and he sat back, staring in Kaia's direction but not focusing on her. His mind was obviously somewhere else.

"Marco, since when do you follow Mexican politics?" Kaia asked. "Since when do you follow *any* politics?"

"Finish the story kid," he snapped, which made me want to punch him. "What happened next?"

Kaia pressed her lips together, composing herself before continuing.

"I tried to get Mom out of there, but she was losing a lot of blood, and she was too heavy to carry, so she gave me her gun." Her gaze darted to me again. "She said to shoot whoever walked through the door."

I couldn't breathe. Kaia clenched and unclenched her hands. I leaned both arms on the table, spent. I think every ounce of my energy was going into my pounding heart.

"Kaia," I whispered.

"I told her I couldn't," Kaia said, her voice faltering. "I told her I didn't want to shoot anyone…that I couldn't…but then she stopped answering me. I thought she'd passed out. Then the door shattered and the gun just…it just went off."

She pressed her lips together, her gaze trained down at the tabletop. I had a feeling that if I touched her, she might crack into a million pieces.

"What happened, *mija*?" Marco asked gently.

"This guy…this boy, really. I mean, he was one of the guys who was after us, but he was only my age… He…he fell into the room. His eyes went wide and then he fell and he…he never got up again."

A tear spilled down her cheek, and she swiped it aside. She looked up at Marco.

"I killed him."

"You had to, kid," Marco said fiercely. "You were protecting your family."

Kaia let out a strained laugh. "Yeah. I did a great job of that."

"Why didn't you tell me?" I asked quietly.

"I didn't want you to know," she said, not looking at me. "I didn't want you to see me that way…as a…a murderer."

"But you aren't a murderer," I told her. "It's like Marco said, you were defending yourself. Protecting your mom."

"It's easy to say that when you weren't there," she told me, closing her eyes. "Sometimes all I can see is that guy's face…"

My throat closed. She was crumbling. I wanted to reach out and take her hand, but her fingertips were digging into her thighs now, the tips curled like claws.

"I used to search the Internet for him," she said, turning to me. "I tried to find boys reported missing in the area. But there were dozens. Dozens of parents trying to find their sons—but none of them were a match."

"That's what it's like there," Marco said. "The country of missing children. Kids get recruited by the cartels or they flee to the United States or they end up…"

"Dead," Kaia finished. The word hit the table like a ten-pound sack of flour.

"What happened next, *mija*?" Marco asked gently.

"Two men walked in. One was Scarface, the guy we saw at the rest stop," she said, her gaze flicking to me. "He was following us back in South Carolina," she told Marco.

"Describe him," Marco prompted.

"Tall, kind of skinny, but strong-looking. He has this horrible scar like this." Kaia drew a line with her finger from her ear to her jaw. Marco's expression hardened. He clearly knew the guy.

"And the other?"

"Very handsome. I remember thinking that even though I was terrified of him. It seemed wrong that someone that good-looking could be so evil. But you could see it in his eyes." Kaia took in a shaky breath. "He crouched in front of Mom and me, but he didn't even look at me. And then he said the weirdest thing."

"What?" Marco asked. "What did he say?"

"He said, 'It's been a long time, Marissa.'"

Marco whispered something in Spanish I didn't understand.

"Marissa, like the—?" I stopped when Kaia narrowed her eyes at me.

"Why would he call her Marissa?" Kaia asked Marco.

Marco pushed back his chair and walked to the back door, staring at his reflection in the glass.

"What's going on, Marco?" Kaia demanded. "Why would that man call Mom Marissa?"

"What happened next?" Marco demanded, turning back to us. "Did he hurt her? Did he take her?"

"I…I don't know," Kaia said, getting up as well. "The man with the scar reached for me, and my mother screamed. That's all I remember. He must have smashed my head against the wall because when I came to I had this throbbing lump on the back of my skull, and everyone was gone. My mother, the men. All that was left of her was this."

She tugged on her locket, and Marco's expression softened.

How could she have kept this from me? How had she been dealing with it alone all this time?

I'd never forget watching my mom slowly slip away, the day my mom left my life. I couldn't imagine what it was like for Kaia, it happening so unexpectedly. So violently.

"Tell me what's going on, Marco," Kaia said. "Do you know these men? Why did they call her Marissa? Was that my mother's real name?"

Suddenly, a shrill beeping sounded upstairs. I startled, thinking it was an alarm—that someone else had tracked us down.

"That's the GPS," Kaia reassured me. "It located my mom's phone."

We both started for the stairs, but Marco didn't move.

"You don't need the GPS," he said. "I know exactly where your mother is."

chapter 22

KAIA

"My mother is a member of a *Mexican drug cartel*?"

I couldn't believe those words had come out of my mouth, let alone that they might be true.

"No. Your mother hated everything the cartel represented, including our father, who ran the whole damn thing."

I had no idea how to process this information. My mother had never talked about her past, except for a few stories here and there. Like the time she'd found a baby lamb that had wandered into the garden outside her bedroom and her mother had let her keep it. Or when Marco had almost drowned in the ocean when he was seven, but a Brazilian movie star had saved him and then given him a kiss. They were always sweet, honey-colored stories that left me feeling as if she'd had a blessed childhood, until her parents had died and she and Marco had come to America.

Which was what she'd always told me had happened.

"So your father…my grandfather…is…?"

"Vincent Quintero Mallorca, the head of the Black Death cartel."

"And he's alive," I said.

"Yes."

"And my mother's real name is Marissa?" I asked.

"No, it's Marisol," Marco said. "But her husband Hector always called her Marissa because that is what our mother called her."

I held on to the back of the nearest chair to keep from blacking out. "Her *husband*?"

"Yes. Her husband. Hector Tinquera. The man my father tapped to take over the cartel once he was gone."

"Hector T.," Oliver said under his breath.

"You heard of him?" Marco demanded, locking a suspicious glare on Oliver.

"There was this guy. He came after us on the road," I explained, my stomach turning as I remembered what I'd done to him. The resistance as the blade entered flesh. "He told us someone named Hector T. had hired him."

"Hector is not a nice guy, *mija*. Your mother was forced to marry him when she was seventeen."

I turned the chair around and fell into it. Oliver moved behind me, but didn't touch me. He seemed very far away. After days of being so close, the distance was conspicuous. He was angry with me or disappointed in me or both. I should never have lied to him. Back at the first safe house in South Carolina—that had been my moment to tell the truth—the whole truth—and I had missed it.

In my mind's eye, I saw Oliver walking away from me,

like he had in Chicago. But this time, when I called out to him, he didn't look back.

"Your dad didn't tap you?" Oliver asked. "Or Kaia's mom?"

Marco chuckled. "A woman would never have been an option for him, and I was only ten years old, not that it's any of your business, Surfer Boy," Marco snapped. "Our father had been getting a lot of death threats and he needed everyone to know who would take over if anything happened to him. Hector was his man."

Marco said this last part to me, clearly irritated by Oliver's presence. There was a bitterness in his tone that I chose to ignore. Marco had always had a questionable set of values. It didn't surprise me that being passed over as head of a multimillion-dollar criminal organization wouldn't have sat well with him. Even if he was still a child at the time.

I had never much liked Uncle Marco, not that I would have ever said it out loud to him or to my mother. I hated the way he treated her—how he was always disappointing her and making her worry. But my mother seemed to have a blind spot when it came to his behavior. No matter what he did, whether it was gamble away all his money or go on a three-week bender, she always forgave him, as long as he came home safe and sound. They shared a love so fierce that watching them together had always made me long for a sibling. They had a shorthand, all these shared memories, all of this history. Mom and Marco would do anything for each other.

"But if Mom was married, how did you guys end up here?" I asked Marco.

He sniffed. "Like I said, Hector was not a nice man. He used to get very jealous when it came to your ma, and he used to take it out on her in ways you don't wanna know about. I tried to protect her once and ended up gettin' my arm broke in three places."

"Oh, God." I was starting to sweat. "This is insane."

What must Oliver think of me? Not only was I a liar and a murderer, but I was a direct descendent of a notorious crime family. Even after everything Oliver had been through, he had a true moral compass. I knew he loved me, but that was before he knew who I really was. Before all of *this*.

Marco cleared his throat. "One night, when I was ten, your mom and Fernanda, my nanny, shook me awake and said we were going. They had already packed our bags. Your ma had found some money—she never would tell me where—and paid somebody to smuggle the three of us over the border. She had just turned eighteen, and she'd had enough of living with that bastard. Once we got to Arizona we stayed with distant relatives of Fernanda, and changed our names… Marisol joined the army to get citizenship and got legal custody of me. The rest you know. Neither your mother nor I have seen Hector T. since."

"Until that day," I finished.

We were all quiet. I was dizzy with the information Marco had dumped on me. My mother had kept so many secrets. Had anything she'd told me about herself, about her childhood, about her life, been true? Had she even really loved my dad? Loved me? Wanted me? Or were we only part of her cover?

"Do you think my father is alive?" I asked shakily.

"Not if Hector T. got to him, *mija*," Marco said quietly. "Your dad could take care a' himself, but Hector T. would've brought an army. He would've seen your dad as the enemy who corrupted his wife. He probably would have—"

"Okay. Okay. I don't need the details." I tried not to imagine what Marco was about to say. Instead I asked, "Why would they have taken a job in Oaxaca? Wouldn't they have known how dangerous it was for Mom to go to Mexico?"

"Your dad...he never knew about your mom's past," Marco told me. "He wouldn't have thought twice."

"But what about her? She could have told him they had to turn down the job. If she'd said no, they'd both be here right now. None of this would have happened."

Oliver's chair made a loud, scraping sound on the tile.

"I don't know what she was thinking," Marco told me, and rubbed his brow. "You'd have to ask her."

There was a moment of suspended silence as I realized I *could* ask her. All of my questions could actually be answered. After all this time trying to accept that she was gone forever...she wasn't.

"You said you knew where she was?"

Hector shoved his hands into the pockets of his black

pants. "If I know Hector, and I know Hector, she's with him. She was his wife. In his mind, she belongs to him forever."

"Okay," Oliver said. His voice startled me. It was quiet, but determined. "So where is Hector?"

"I heard that he set up shop north of the border a couple years back," Marco said. "Came here to strengthen the Black Cartel's presence in the good old USA."

"Where?" I asked.

"Out in LA, I can find the exact address with a coupla texts. I still know a guy," Marco said, seeming proud of this fact. "But I don't recommend you go after him, kid. You're lucky he left you alive the first time you two crossed paths."

"No way," I said, rising on shaky knees. "If my mother is alive, I'm going to find her. I'm going to bring her home. We were a family. A team. It's what my father would do."

In the back of my mind, all I could hear was my mother's voice. *Never stop fighting*, mija.

I didn't care that she'd told me to stay away. I needed to know that I was still her little girl, her Kiki. I needed my mom.

"We're going to LA," I said.

"Kaia," Oliver said. I gathered my courage and looked him dead in the eye. His expression was hard. "Can I talk to you for a sec?" he asked, and his gaze flicked at Marco. "Alone?"

chapter 23

OLIVER

"ACTUALLY." KAIA PAUSED. "MARCO AND I HAVE A LOT OF CATCH-ing up to do."

"It'll only take a second," I said, grinding my teeth. Though that was clearly a lie. After the conversation we'd just had and all the new information swirling like a tornado inside my brain, I wasn't sure which way was up.

"Oliver, please… Why don't you go back up to bed?" Kaia suggested, nailing the lid to my coffin. "I'll be up soon."

And that was it. I'd been dismissed. I glanced at Marco. His smirk said it all. I had been replaced by a paunchy, aging relative. She had her uncle to help her. She was going to get her family back. And she didn't need me anymore.

"Fine," I said.

I walked up the stairs like I hadn't been slighted, but by the time I got to the top, I felt sick. My entire life was slipping through my fingers, and there was nothing I could do to stop it.

I paused outside Kaia's pink travesty of a room. Where we'd kissed this afternoon and passed out in each other's arms

only a couple of hours ago. Everything had changed so quickly—
I'd felt so close to her then, and now she'd rejected me. I couldn't
go back in there. I hovered in the doorway, frozen with indeci-
sion. Then I saw the blue glow emanating through the door of her
parents' bedroom. *The Batcave.*

We hadn't cleaned up the mess Kaia had made during her
fit, and we hadn't gone back to close the doors to the supersecret
room, either. I had a feeling Kaia wouldn't want me going in there
without her, but at the moment, I didn't care.

Sure enough, the map on the computer screen had a
pulsating dot over Southern California. Kaia's gun was on the
table next to the keyboard. I picked it up—it was heavier than
it looked—and squinted one eye to stare down the sight line. I
caught my reflection in one of the glass cases. Robin hadn't had
time to cut my hair since before school started, and it had gotten
long over the past few weeks. Some of my freshly cleaned curls
had dried into ringlets. Surfer Boy? I looked more like a six-year-
old girl. No wonder Marco wasn't taking me seriously.

I put the gun down and backed up to get a better look at
myself, running my hands over my hair. My elbow hit a speaker
on the wall and suddenly, the Batcave filled with voices.

"...dead meat, kid," Marco was saying.

"He's my boyfriend, Marco," Kaia replied. "He's coming
with us."

My heart stopped. *What?*

"Please? That kid? Not only will he get himself killed, but
he'll get you killed too."

My jaw clenched so tightly I swear I heard a tooth crack.

"He's tougher than he looks," Kaia said.

"First of all, no," Marco said with a laugh in his voice. "And secondly, tough's got nothing to do with it. He's not one of us. This kind of thing, you keep it in the family."

"He *is* family," Kaia replied.

I squared my shoulders a little. Maybe all wasn't lost.

"No. He's not. He's not blood. And he never will be. The sooner you figure that out the better."

I waited for Kaia to defend me again. And I waited. My fingers curled into fists. The hum of the computer towers was deafening. There was a hitch in the back of my throat.

Say something. Say anything.

But she didn't. I reached up and clicked off the intercom.

On one of the monitors, a search bar was open, the cursor blinking. *ENTER NAME*: read the prompt.

He's not blood. And he never will be.

I was already typing before I fully realized what I was doing.

VICTOR MICHAEL LANGE

A dozen photos popped up on the screen. My father's was the third one. He looked older. Scruffier. He had my same blond curls and a reddish-blond goatee, which I'd never seen. But it was him. I sat and clicked on his picture. A record of his last few residences scrolled in front of me. They matched up perfectly with the post marks on my birthday cards. A year in Virginia, a couple in New York, about a year and a half in Chicago, and on and on. It was his current residence that made me gag. He was living in Charleston. Not ten miles from Robin's house. *The man practically lived down the street from me and had never even come by to say hello.*

My hands clenched atop the desk.

He's not blood.

What the hell did blood matter? It didn't. Not one goddamned bit.

I cleared the computer screen. I never wanted to lay eyes on that asshole's face again.

I walked back into Kaia's parents' bedroom, still seething. There was no way Kaia would leave me behind. No freaking way. On some level, I understood that Marco was necessary. He knew these people, the cartel, and would know how to deal with them. But she loved me. We were family.

Or—there was always an or—maybe I'd been right all along. Maybe I wasn't good enough for this version of Kaia. And Marco was sitting in the kitchen, hammering that point home.

I walked around the end of the bed, stepping over crumpled sweaters and balled-up socks. Near the edge of the large dresser was a framed picture of Kaia's dad with three other soldiers. They all wore green camouflage gear and bullet-proof vests. Her dad held a nasty-looking rifle in front of him with both hands. His blond hair had been shorn tight to his head and sweat sheened his lip and brow. There was a scowl on his face that would have made any intelligent enemy throw up his hands in surrender. The man was hardcore.

No wonder Kaia was as strong and brave as she was.

If her mother was half as cool as she'd made her out to be, Kaia basically had the combined DNA of a superhero. And I had the DNA of a deadbeat jackass and sweet woman who'd died young of cancer.

I glanced in the mirror above the dresser, then turned and walked into the bathroom. I found what I needed in the bottom drawer.

Marco thought I wasn't good enough? He wanted to convince Kaia to leave me behind? Well, we'd see about that.

chapter 24

KAIA

"WHO THE HELL DO YOU THINK YOU ARE?" I SNAPPED.

My words hung in the air. A darkness fell across Marco's face, as if he'd pulled a mask down over his eyes.

"What did you say to me?"

"I said, who the hell do you think you are?" I stood up fast, knocking my chair over with a clatter, and glared down at him. "You can't tell me what to do. You can't tell me who to leave behind. Some family. You broke my mother's heart more times than I can count."

"You are way outta line, kid." Marco got up and jammed a stubby finger in my direction. "Respect your elders."

"Sorry, but people need to *earn* respect." I stalked to the refrigerator to have something to do, somewhere to focus my kinetic energy. I could barely contain my rage as I grabbed a glass and filled it with water from the door dispenser.

"Who do you think has been here taking care a' this place?" he whisper-shouted. "You think I *wanted* to be here? You think I like living in boring-ass Houston?"

"It's gotta be better than Reno," I spat back, slamming the glass onto the counter so hard water sloshed onto the marble. "Tell me, how much of my parents' money have you lost to random thugs over the years? Tens of thousands? Hundreds? You'd disappear for weeks at a time, leaving my mom worrying by the phone. A couple years ago she lost twenty pounds thinking you had to be dead somewhere, and the whole time you were in Vegas partying like some reality show has-been."

Marco's eyes narrowed. "She told you all that?"

"She told me everything," I said. "Everything I wanted to know, anyway. That's how the three of us worked."

At least, that was how I thought our family worked. I had thought my parents had always been honest with me—until my mother's text a couple days ago and the can of worms it had opened and then dumped over my head.

"I don't trust you, Marco. And I'm not going to leave Oliver behind because you want to be the conquering hero, riding in to save my mom or whatever."

"I'm not going to even dignify that with a response," Marco spat. "I love your mother more than I love life itself. You think I don't know I've been a disappointment to her? You think I haven't spent the last year praying to Jesus that she'd come home so I could say I'm sorry? I owe my existence to your ma, and I'd do anything for her." He paused, then said quietly, "And I'd do anything for you because you're her daughter." He shook his head, and sighed. "You want to bring him? Fine. Then his blood is on your hands."

I refused to let Marco see that he'd rattled me. I took a long drink of water, then put the glass down. "Always so dramatic, huh, Marco?"

"Dramatic?" he blurted, his face screwed up in indignation. "You want to talk dramatic? How about the time Hector Tinquera cut a twelve-year-old boy's fingers off one by one because his father had borrowed a car and neglected to return it at the designated time?"

My stomach turned. Marco took a step closer to me and pressed a finger to my temple. "How about the fact that Hector shot his own *mother* in the head when he found out she'd kissed a man who wasn't his father?"

I tilted my head away. "You're exaggerating," I said, but my voice had no strength to it.

Marco leaned in to me, so close I could smell the chicken soup on his breath.

"How about the fact that the first time your mother got pregnant, he forced her to have an abortion when he found out it wasn't a boy?"

Marco's good eye trembled in its socket. The other seemed to stare at some fixed point somewhere off my right shoulder.

"What?" I gasped.

"They had to have six men hold her down to drug her, *mija*. After that, she didn't come out of her room for three months."

"No." Tears filled my eyes as I shook my head. "There's no way."

"I'm telling you, *Kiki*, this man is ruthless. And if he sees how you feel about that blond pinup boy of yours, he will not hesitate to slaughter him. No. He'll torture him until he's *begging* to be slaughtered. That's who Hector T. is."

Marco turned away from me and wiped his mouth with one hand. "It's bad enough you're taking your own life in your hands, kid. Don't be responsible for his."

He walked toward the living room and paused, his hands on either side of the doorjamb. His head bowed away from me.

"Whatever you think of me, I *am* glad to see you." He glanced back and smiled slightly. "Let's leave first thing in the morning."

Then he was gone. I sank to the floor, covered my face with my hands, and cried. I cried for my mother—for everything she'd been put through when she was my age. I cried for my father, not daring to imagine what Hector T. might have done to him. And I cried for myself, for the impossible decision I was about to make.

chapter 25

OLIVER

THE SUN BLINDED ME THE MOMENT I OPENED MY EYES. A DOOR slammed, and I sat up, heart in my throat. I'd fallen asleep in Kaia's parents' bed. What time was it? I reached for my back pocket and my phone, but there was no back pocket, no phone. I was still wearing Kaia's dad's pajama pants.

An engine revved, and I threw myself out of bed, sprinting for the stairs.

Nononononononono—

I raced outside and caught Kaia halfway to a beat up red truck, which I had to assume was Marco's. It had already been loaded with duffel bags, probably full of bulletproof vests, automatic weapons, and half the spy paraphernalia in the Batcave. How I wished I wasn't such a heavy sleeper. They'd snuck out all that contraband right under my snoring nose. I grabbed Kaia's arm. She stiffened as she turned.

"Really?" I blurted. "You were just going to leave me here?"

Kaia's eyes flicked toward the house. Uncle Marco leaned against the wall, smoking a cigarette.

"I left you a note," she said meekly. Then, she blinked.

"By the way, what happened to your hair?"

My hand instinctively went to my head. It felt like soft peach fuzz. Did I really think a haircut was gonna make a badass?

"Kaia," I protested. "There's no way I'm—"

"Well, hello there!"

The front door of the neighboring house creaked open, and a woman in a pink sweat suit stepped outside. She had curly white hair and glasses that took up most of her small face.

"Kaia! Oh, I thought that was you! It's so good to see you."

Kaia looked caught, and I saw her battling with herself. Ignore the sweet old lady or not? She chose the latter.

"Hi, Mrs. Appleby."

Kaia walked over to the waist-high fence between their properties, where the woman met her. The old lady reached her thin arms over and enveloped Kaia in a hug.

"Where have you been, dear? It's been ages!"

"I've been around," Kaia said vaguely. "How are you? How's Mr. Wilson?"

"Oh, he's fine!" Mrs. Appleby laughed and gestured at her porch. "As fat and lazy as ever."

I assumed she was talking about the obese orange cat that took up most of the top step. Awesome. We were right in the middle of a life-defining throw down, and now Kaia was discussing a cat?

"And who's this?" Mrs. Appleby asked, gesturing toward me.

"I'm Oliver, Mrs. Appleby. Nice to meet you," I said, forcing a smile.

"You as well." She gave Kaia a conspiratorial look. "He's very handsome. Good for you!"

Kaia hesitated. "Thank you. It was good to see you, Mrs. Appleby, but we really have to get going."

We. Yeah, right.

"He looks a lot like your father, you know," Mrs. Appleby said, as if Kaia hadn't spoken. "Girls go for boys who remind them of their dads. Say hi to your dad for me. I saw him a couple of days ago in the backyard, but he was in such a rush. He didn't stop over to say hello."

The color drained from Kaia's face. "What?"

"Your father. He was on his cell phone," Mrs. Appleby said. "He didn't seem happy. Young people today are always so stressed."

Marco crushed his cigarette under his boot and walked over to the fence.

"You must mean my uncle, Marco," Kaia said, though her hand was unsteady as she gestured at him. "He's been working on the yard."

Mrs. Appleby's eyes narrowed behind her thick glasses. "No, no. Your father. Blond hair, tall. Has that tattoo on the back of his neck. Some kind of Gaelic religious symbol."

"Thor's hammer," Kaia breathed.

"What?" Mrs. Appleby and I said at the same time.

"It's not Gaelic, it's from a comic book" Kaia fished in her pocket and produced the keys to the demolished Honda we'd left on the road back in Illinois.

"This?" she said, holding out the key chain to Mrs. Appleby.

"Yes! That's it! Believe me, I know your father when I see him."

Kaia reached for my arm. Finding out one dead parent was alive was a lot to take in, but possibly two?

"I'm sorry, when was this?" Kaia asked.

"A couple of days ago. Must've been…Saturday, maybe?" Mrs. Appleby mused. "Yes, that was it, because I was watering my hydrangeas, and I always water my hydrangeas on Saturday."

A phone rang. Mrs. Appleby turned toward her house. "Oh, I'd better get that. The vet's calling today with some test results. Mr. Wilson's diabetes, you know. Terrible thing. But he's a trooper. Don't be a stranger, dear!"

"I won't," Kaia muttered.

The woman carefully climbed the stairs, stepped over Mr. Wilson, and disappeared inside.

Kaia looked up at me, still pale. "Do you think—"

"The woman's clearly confused, Kaia," Uncle Marco said, before I could get a word in. "She probably saw a blond meter guy. Or she's remembering your dad from years ago. Come on. Let's get a move on already. If you want me to drive you to your funeral, I'd like to get it over with."

He walked around to the driver's side and got into the truck, slamming the door so hard the whole vehicle shook.

"You coming?" he asked.

Kaia nodded absently and reached for the door.

"Wait. Wait for me to get dressed," I said. "I'll be back in two minutes."

"I can't," she said, her eyes filled with tears. She looked at me and cleared her throat, then repeated more resolutely. "I can't, Oliver. If everything goes okay, I'll call you. The house phone works."

"You expect me to stay here? To hang out here and wait?"

"You don't have to." She got in the car and slammed the door. "But I hope you will." She shot me an apologetic look. "There's money on the table with the note."

I scoffed. Did she think the money would somehow make this okay? Then Marco put the truck in reverse and pulled out of the driveway.

"Don't do this," I called after them. "Don't go!"

But the truck didn't slow. All I could do was stand there and watch as the rear bumper grew smaller in the shimmering heat of the morning.

18 MONTHS AGO

IT WAS CLEAR FROM THE MOMENT I WOKE UP THAT I WAS ALONE. MY
mother was gone. The men were gone. My dad hadn't returned.
I wanted to wait for him, but my mother had told me he wasn't
coming back, and if I was going to run, it had to be now. The motel
rooms had been shot to holy hell. The police would be coming soon.

I pushed myself up, tears streaming down my face, and saw
stars. The back of my head throbbed and my eyes burned like
they'd been skewered with knitting needles. There was blood everywhere. My mother's blood. The blood of the boy I'd—

My gaze settled on the wall to where the bullet had lodged
itself near the door trim. It had gone straight through the boy's chest.

I somehow made it to the toilet before throwing up.
Afterward, I rinsed my face with two shaking hands, and stared
into the mirror. I was a mess. Blood on my shirt and in my hair,
waxy skin, red eyes. I had to get my shit together.

"You know what to do, right, Kiki?"

I did. And I wasn't going to let my mother down. Not now.
Not again.

I staggered to my closet and pulled out my bag, changing into a clean shirt and pulling my hair under a baseball cap. Then I went to the safe in my parents' room to retrieve our passports—all Austrian—and my parents' corresponding driver's licenses.

Shaking, I knew I'd have to dispose of my parents' fake documents. No one could ever know that they'd been here.

When I surveyed the damage, my eyes brimmed. My mother's blood was all over the floor. She had been here. But where was she now? Was she alive? What had those men done to her?

I saw something glint out of the corner of my eye and bent to retrieve my mother's locket. Inside the small gold heart was a picture of me, age three, and a picture of my father. I shoved it in my pocket, grabbed the Batphone and Sophia off the floor, and walked out into the blazing sunshine.

I deposited their passports, one by one, in various garbage cans across Oaxaca, and outside a small café, I finally disposed of the phone. After walking a few blocks, I found a pay phone with a fogged glass shield leaning at a precarious angle. When I picked up the receiver, I was surprised to hear a dial tone.

My heart pounded as I connected to an operator and told her in Spanish that I wanted to call a United States number, collect.

The phone rang four times. Then a gruff man's voice sounded over the line. "Hello?"

The operator told him in halting English that his grand-daughter was calling collect from Mexico. I held my breath. He accepted the charges.

"Hello?" he said again, more gently this time.

I delivered the line I had hoped I'd never have to use. "I miss you, Grandpa."

There was a pause, and tears rolled down my cheeks.

"Then it's time to come home."

chapter 26

KAIA

Slamming the car door in Oliver's face was like slamming my bedroom door on my parents after our stupid argument last year. I'd never be able to take back the finality of it.

"As soon as we find your mother, I'm going to apologize," Marco was saying. "I'm going to make it up to her. Everything. I swear it. I still can't believe that she's alive."

The second we were free of the driveway, my life flashed before my eyes. But it wasn't my entire life. It was just my life with Oliver. Swimming in the ocean at Folly Beach, sharing a hot chocolate after a soccer game, laying in the sun behind the school while he stroked my hair away from my forehead. Oliver's smile, Oliver's hands, Oliver's bruises, Oliver's profile, Oliver's muddy cleats, his wrinkled T-shirts, his blue and white backpack, his knuckles and freckles and earlobes and curls.

I started to hyperventilate. I tried to take a normal breath, but I couldn't. My chest was so tight I may as well have been crushed under the weight of a thousand cars.

"If I get a shot at Hector T., I swear to you, I'm going to make him pay," Marco rambled.

He looked at me like I was supposed to respond to what he was saying, but I couldn't focus.

Oliver was never going to forgive me, and I couldn't blame him. He'd been there for me through everything. Even though I'd lied to him. Even though I'd kept secrets from him. Even though I'd almost abandoned him in the middle of nowhere—not that he knew about that, but it was possible he suspected.

Yet he still loved me. He was still willing to risk his life for me. I couldn't, fucking, breathe.

"You okay, kid?" Marco asked, pressing on the brakes to come to a stop at the intersection at the end of our road. "It's okay, you did the right thing."

"I can't," I whined, doubling over at the waist. "I can't."

"Come on, kid. Get it together," Marco said, reaching over to rub my back. "Breathe. Just breathe!"

I was starting to see spots. "We…go back…," I sputtered. "We…haveto…goback!"

I looked up to plead with him as my vision grayed over. The front grill of a huge Hummer was gunning right for the driver's side of the truck. I screamed with all the air left in my lungs and then, I was flying.

chapter 27

OLIVER

It sounded like two freight trains colliding, even from a good quarter mile away. The truck hurtled into the air, flipped over, and landed upside down. Then, with a wail, it tilted sideways and slid down the embankment at the side of the road before ever so slowly flipping again and landing back on its wheels. The Hummer that had hit them sat there, blocking both lanes. There wasn't another car on the road.

"Kaia!" I screamed.

I took off, running down the center of the scalding blacktop in my bare feet. I was a few yards away when a man with the build of a WWE wrestler got out of the Hummer—which barely looked dinged—and slid down the slope toward Marco's truck.

Who the hell was this now? Some other enemy of Kaia's parents? How did they keep finding us? Not that it mattered if Kaia was already dead.

The man yanked open the driver's side door. I ran down the hill and went to the passenger door. All I could think about was getting Kaia out of there before this guy grabbed her.

"Kaia!"

The wrestler glanced at me. He looked confused. Then he clutched Marco by the front of his shirt with both hands and dragged him out of the car.

"Kaia!" I shouted again.

She blinked a few times before her eyes finally focused. There was a gash across her hairline, leaking blood down her forehead and nose.

"What happened?" she asked.

"You were in an accident," I said, trying to be calm. "Can you move?"

She nodded and slumped toward the door, then cried out in pain.

"What?" I blurted. "What is it?"

"My ankle! I can't turn my ankle!"

At that moment, Marco came careening toward us, his head slamming against the side of the truck as he fell to the ground.

Kaia yelped in surprise. "Marco!"

The wrestler dude wasn't done with him yet. He picked up Marco, propped him against the side of the truck like a rag doll and pulled back a fist.

"Leave him alone!" Kaia shouted. "He didn't do anything to you!"

The wrestler looked inside the cab and laughed.

"Darlin', you got no clue what you're talking about."

Then he slammed his boulder-sized fist into Marco's jaw. Blood spurted everywhere. I opened Kaia's door. Her ankle was wedged underneath a jumble of broken dashboard plastic and metal.

"We have to get you out of here."

"Oliver, no. You have to run," Kaia whimpered. "This has nothing to do with you."

"See, that's your main problem," I said, as the whole truck shook with Marco hitting its side again. "You've yet to figure out anything to do with you has everything to do with me."

She managed a smile as a drop of blood dripped off the end of her nose. I bent into the truck and pulled at the plastic casing closest to her ankle, prying it away half an inch. Kaia jimmied her ankle free, then winced.

"Is it broken?" I asked.

"I don't think so. But it hurts. A lot."

"C'mere."

I wrapped my arms around her and pulled her out of the truck. She hopped away from the door on her good foot, and together we made our way around the front. Blood from Kaia's forehead splattered my white T-shirt.

"Stop!" Kaia shouted, when she saw the man cocking his fist again. Marco's face looked like hamburger meat. Rotten hamburger meat. "If you want to take me back to Hector T. or whoever it is you're working for, I'll go! Marco has nothing to do with it!"

"Girl, I got no idea who Hector T. is, or who you are for that matter." The wrestler let Marco side to the ground in a heap. "What I *do* know is that Marco here owes me ten large, and it's way past due."

Kaia glared down at her sputtering uncle. "Is this your *bookie*?"

"I thought you were giving me another week," Marco said, trying to push himself up by gripping the front tire.

"That was two weeks ago!" the man shouted.

"This is unbelievable." Kaia extricated herself from my arms and tried to walk back to her side of the truck, but fell sideways against the grill. "Shit."

"What do you need?" I asked her.

"My backpack." She turned so her back was against the car and ran her arm over her forehead, smearing the blood into her hair. She kept her right knee bent, holding her foot off the grass. "Get my backpack. Please."

I reached inside the open cab and pulled out the gray backpack. Kaia ripped it open.

"You want ten grand? Here." She fumbled a stack of bills from the bag and slammed it against the man's sizable chest. Guess there'd been another stash of cash in the Batcave. "Here's ten grand. Plus interest!"

The bookie's eyes widened. He sized up the backpack covetously, realizing that there had to be more money inside. On impulse, I reached into the bag and slipped out Kaia's gun, aiming it at the man's chest in what I hoped was a convincing way.

"Oliver!" Kaia cried.

"Whatever you're thinking, don't," I said through gritted teeth. "You got what you came for, and my guess is someone on this street has already called the cops thanks to the mess you made. I'd quit while you're ahead."

The bookie raised his hands. "You make a good point, kid."

Then he turned tail and ran for his tanklike vehicle. I lowered the gun and shoved it back in the bag.

"Wow," Kaia said. "That was pretty intense, Oliver."

The look of admiration in her eyes pissed me off. Five minutes ago she was walking away like she didn't need me. Well, look where we were now.

"I'll be right back," I said, starting up the embankment.

"Where're you going?" Kaia asked.

"To get your dad's car," I said without pausing. "Not like I can single-handedly carry both of you back to the house. At least not before the cops get here."

I tried not to think about my bare feet or the bloodstained pajamas I was wearing as I stormed indignantly up the road.

chapter 28

KAIA

"WHAT NOW?"

Oliver situated himself as far away from me as he could and still be in the kitchen. He'd cleaned up Marco to the best of his abilities using the extensive first aid kit my parents kept in the hall closet, and wrapped my ankle in ice and an ACE Bandage. The cut on my head I'd taken care of myself. I couldn't stand Oliver's cold, businesslike demeanor. Not that I could blame him. Maybe if Marco and I had turned back to the house in time—if I'd apologized and told him I'd wanted him to come with us... But I hadn't gotten that chance, and now he was furious.

At least it didn't seem like I was going to need stitches. Butterfly bandages had stopped the bleeding. But Marco and I looked like we'd been through a war.

"We take my dad's car," I said, shifting in my seat. My ankle was resting on a second chair and my leg was starting to get stiff.

Marco shook head, then winced. "Not a good idea. You

got all these people looking for you, you can bet they know what kinds of cars your mom and dad drove. They might even have the plate numbers or be able to track the GPS. It'll just make you easier to find."

Oliver blew out a sigh. "You don't have another safe house nearby with extra cars parked in its garage?" He sounded half-amused, half-resigned A sudden rush of endorphins killed my pain and I sat up straighter. We didn't have any other safe houses nearby—unless one considered Sante Fe, New Mexico close—but we *did* have another transportation option. Although, with my ankle, the plan was iffy at best.

"What?" Oliver asked. "What is it?"

I looked at him and smiled, hoping he'd smile back. He didn't. Still, there was no turning back now.

"I think I have an idea."

⬤

The concrete and ammonia scent of the Go Go Storage facility reminded me of my dad more vividly than his bedroom or a whiff of the shirts in his closet. We used to come here every weekend when we were in Houston, and each time it felt like Christmas morning.

I grinned at Oliver. "You ready to meet the rest of my family?"

"Kaia, please tell me you haven't been keeping your parents locked in there all this time," he said, looking tired.

I clenched my jaw and stooped to grasp the metal

handle on the orange, garage style door—gripping Oliver's elbow for balance. I flung open the door. It retracted noisily, clanging to a stop, and there they were. Betty and Bettina. The family motorcycles.

"Oh, baby, it is *so* good to see you," I murmured.

With Oliver's help, I limped up next to Bettina, my 2012 Triumph Street Triple, all black, with chrome accents, and ran my hand over the supple leather seat. She was perfect, her silver muffler glinting in the sunlight. I kicked my bad leg over her and settled down onto her seat. The sigh that escaped my lips was pure joy. But there was something else too. I felt a certainty pulse through me. I was doing the right thing. Maybe it was seeing our bikes, all shined up and ready to go, as if we'd never left. Maybe it was the fact that everything about this storage space *was* my father, from the oil stain under my boot to the boxes of old CDs in the corner to the superhero movie posters lining the walls. I knew he was watching over me, and I knew what he'd want me to do.

I had to find my mom. We had to be a family again, to whatever extent we could be. No matter what her text said.

"Um, Kaia?" Oliver said. "Is your plan really to ride motorcycles all the way to LA?"

"That's my plan," I said, running my fingertips reverently over Bettina's handlebars. I looked at Marco. "Can you grab the key?"

Moving slowly thanks to the beat-down he'd suffered at the hands of his bookie, Marco retrieved the key from its hook on the pegboard. I shoved it into the slot and turned, then pushed the stop switch and starter button. My baby roared to life, and exhilaration flooded my bones. Then, I tried to shift into first.

"Shit!" I cried out. My ankle was gripped with pain.

"What are you thinking? You can't use that ankle," Marco chided.

"I know. I know." I leaned down to grip it as it throbbed. "Wishful thinking."

"So now what?" Oliver asked as I cut the engine again.

"You drive Bettina here and I'll ride behind you," I told him.

Oliver laughed humorlessly and raised his palms. "Are you kidding me? We'd both be killed. I don't know how to ride a motorcycle!"

"So I'll teach you."

I reached for his hand and awkwardly climbed off the bike, trying not to jostle my ankle too much.

"Marco can ride Big Betty, and we can shove the bags in her side car."

I tilted my head toward my dad's Harley. It was a lot more bike than Bettina, but even in his debilitated state, Marco could handle her. As long as his good eye didn't swell shut.

Letting go of Oliver, I hopped over to Big Betty and checked the gas gage. It was full, like Bettina's. That was so dad. He was always prepared. We'd be good to go for a couple hundred miles.

"Is this why I'm still here?" Oliver asked.

My heart skipped a beat at his tone. He crossed his arms over his chest and stared me down. I still couldn't get over his new haircut. If he'd looked older and hotter a couple of days ago, now he was a supermodel. It was very distracting. Especially when he so clearly hated my guts.

"What do you mean?" I asked.

"This morning you were ready to ditch me, but now you're hurt, and you need me again," Oliver said. "Tell me the truth, Kaia. If you hadn't wrenched your ankle in that crash, would I even be here right now?"

Marco muttered something about a smoke and made his way outside. I limped back over to Bettina and gripped her handlebar and seat for support. She was all that separated me from Oliver, but she may as well have been an army tank.

"Oliver, I'm sorry," I told him. "I was coming back for you, I swear. Right before that asshole drove into us, I was telling Marco to turn around. We were going to come back for you."

There was a spark of hope in Oliver's eyes, but he bowed his head, and then his stone-cold expression was back. "How am I supposed to believe you? How am I supposed to trust anything you say to me ever again?"

"I'm sorry I lied about that day in Oaxaca. About my parents. About everything, okay?" I begged. "Please, just don't hate me."

"You don't get it," Oliver said.

"No, *you* don't get it." My voice broke and I paused, trying to pull myself together. "I have relived that day a million times since it happened, Oliver, and not only asking myself what I could have done differently. Could I have saved my mom if I'd...done *anything* at all? But that guy...the guy I killed...I see his face every single time I close my eyes. The way he looked at me, like he didn't understand what was happening to him..."

I pressed the heels of my hands to my brow bone and squeezed my eyes shut, trying to clear the boy's image, but there it was, bright as day. My eyes filled with hot tears.

"I can't get him out of my head no matter what I do!" I whispered harshly. "And talking about it? It makes it worse."

"Kaia—"

"And the way you're looking at me right now doesn't help either," I muttered. "Can't we just—"

"Kaia, stop." Oliver's eyes shone. "I'm not mad at you because you didn't tell me the details of the worst fucking day of your life. I get you not wanting to relive that. I haven't told you what it was like to watch my mom die, have I? How I felt the day my dad walked out of social services and drove away? Or the way my skin split open the first time Jack hit me? No. I don't need to know the gory details of your worst moments any more than you need to know mine."

He walked around Bettina and stopped in front of me. "But I need to know is the big stuff. The stuff that makes you,

you." He reached out for my cold, clammy hand and held it gently. "Because I love you. Every. Last. Little. Damaged. Bit of you."

He kissed a different part of my face with each word. One cheek, then the other, then my forehead, my nose, my chin.

"Why did they do this, Oliver?" I heard myself say.

"Who do what?" he asked.

"My parents. Why did they drag me around the world while they committed *murder* for a *living*? Who does that? What kind of people are they? What kind of parents? Why couldn't I have had a normal life? Why didn't they love me enough to give me a normal life?"

I felt the tears coming and bowed my head against his shoulder, biting them back. Oliver hugged me, rubbing his hand up and down my back.

"Maybe they wanted to give you a normal life, you know? Maybe they wanted to, but they didn't know how. Maybe that's not who they were."

I took in a broken breath. "Sometimes I think you're way too mature for your own good."

"It's a gift," he replied, straight-faced. "And a burden."

I laughed. He smirked and kissed my forehead.

"But I get it," he said. "You think I don't have a thousand 'whys' in my head all the time? Why did my mother have to die? Why did my dad have to leave me? Why did I get dumped into Robin's crappy life? Why does Trevor have to deal with all the shit he has to deal with? Why does Jack even exist? Oh,

236 | KIERAN SCOTT

and get this—why has my dad been living in Charleston for the past year but has never even come to see me?"

"What?" I felt as if I'd had the wind knocked out of me. "How do you—"

"I looked him up on your Batcave's supercomputer," he said. "And now I have one more big, fat 'why' to add to the list."

My heart felt sick for him. How could his father not want Oliver in his life? He had no clue how amazing his own son was and he didn't even care.

"I've asked myself all these questions a million times, Kaia, but now, I think I finally have the answers."

I sniffled. "You do?"

"Because," he said, running his hand over my hair. "If we didn't have such fucked up lives, we never would have found each other."

All the tension in my body finally released. He was right. Blissfully, beautifully, perfectly right. If my parents hadn't disappeared, I never would have ended up in South Carolina. If his mother hadn't gotten cancer and his dad hadn't left him, he never would have moved in with Robin and lived in our town or gone to our school.

Maybe fate really had screwed with us to bring us together. It wasn't pretty, but it made us, us.

"I like that answer," I said with a smile. We kissed, a long, slow, comforting, exciting kiss that lasted until Marco cleared his throat and crushed his cigarette under his boot right outside the door.

"So," Oliver said, pulling back. "How about you teach me how to ride this thing?"

"Bettina," I said with mock admonishment. "Her name is Bettina."

chapter 29

OLIVER

EL PASO, TEXAS. ONE MORE TOWN I NEVER THOUGHT I'D SEE. I lifted the helmet off my sweaty head and took in the mountains sprawling in the distance. Before this trip, I'd never seen a mountain in my life. Not in person anyway. Now, after Kentucky, southern Illinois, and western Texas, I was starting to get used to them.

I took a deep breath as Kaia let go of my waist and hoisted herself off the bike. I reached for her hand, and she squeezed mine, then started limping toward the motel where Marco had already disappeared inside.

I put the kickstand down and followed her. After ten hours in the saddle with only two quick food breaks, my whole body felt like it was buzzing. The vibrations of the road had moved into my bones, and every step I took was an effort. The muscles on the insides of my thighs would never be the same again.

But still, I was in love—utterly and completely—with riding. I had a feeling that driving in a car would never feel right to me again. Not that I could afford a bike of my own any more than I could get my own ass to the DMV to get an actual license, but hey, maybe someday. Out on the road, anything seemed possible.

I'm never going back.

The thought came out of nowhere, but it filled me with this lighter-than-air feeling. I looked around at the mountains and I felt sure. Knowing I could bump into my dad on the street in Charleston was even more of an incentive to stay away. I would miss Trevor. I would always think of him and always hope and pray that he was safe, but that part of my life was over.

The only question was, where the hell would I end up?

Kaia pulled off her helmet. Her short blond hair swung. What I would have given to run my fingers through it. To get her alone for five minutes. To talk about how she imagined our future. But then Marco reappeared, and I remembered it wasn't just Kaia and me anymore.

"I got us a room," Marco said, striding across the parking lot.

"Just one?" I asked, which made Kaia blush.

Marco flipped the key around on its silver ring. "I don't think we should split up. Besides, I wanna keep an eye on you two."

He narrowed his eyes as he looked at me, and I raised my hands. I was too tired to deal with his pseudofather bullshit.

"Whatever," I muttered. "All I want is some food and a bed."

"And that bed's gonna be shared with me," Marco said, crooking his arm around my neck. "Fair warning, kid. I like my space."

Whoop-de-frickin'-do. Marco dragged me toward room five

of the ten-room establishment. The outer walls were a dingy poop color, and the doors had been painted gray. The hotel was located about fifty yards from where two freeways intersected, and tractor-trailers blew by at alarming speeds, kicking up discarded food wrappers and flattening the grass with their exhaust. It was not going to be a quiet night, but if I was going to be sharing a bed with Uncle Marco, I had a feeling noise was going to be the least of my problems.

Inside, the room was small, dark, and wood-paneled with a popcorn ceiling and a threadbare rug. The two double beds sagged in the middle, and there was one table lamp to light the room. Kaia limped to the bathroom and shoved the shower curtain aside.

"I got dibs!" she announced, and closed the door.

I collapsed facedown on the nearest bed, then smelled the comforter, and rolled onto my back, coughing out the stench. Marco stared at me.

"So, what're your intentions with my niece?"

My heart thumped. The water turned on inside the bathroom, so at least Kaia couldn't hear this conversation. "My intentions? At this point? To keep her alive."

"What about after that?" Marco asked, shoving his hands into his pockets.

"What do you mean? Like, am I going to marry her?" I asked. "We're seventeen."

Obviously I'm going to marry her.

"Look, kid. Her heart's already been broken wide open, so I wanna know if you're gonna break it even more."

"No. Are you kidding? If anything, she's gonna break mine," I said.

As soon as the words were out of my mouth, I wished I could swallow them back. This was what came of total exhaustion—my brain was having a hard time keeping up with my mouth.

"What makes you say that?" Marco asked.

I pushed myself off the mattress and walked toward the window, my leg muscles screaming. The parking lot was full of cars, but there was no one in sight. "Look, man. We're going to find her mom. Once they're reunited, the two of them will go off together, right? Back to Houston or somewhere else. Where am I supposed to fit in to that picture?"

"Hey. I heard the girl promise she'd never leave your sorry ass. You think she's gonna abandon you after that?" Marco asked, sounding offended. "You think she'd renege on a promise? It's not in her DNA."

I looked down at the floor, and my heart felt heavy. Kaia and I could make all the romantic promises to each other that we wanted, but it didn't change reality. What was I going to do? Go live with Kaia and her mom wherever they settled down? Somehow I had a feeling that wasn't going to fly. Whose parents wanted their daughter to have a live-in boyfriend?

"I'm not sure she's gonna have a choice," I said.

chapter 30

KAIA

WHEN I WOKE UP, THE LEATHER GLOVE OVER MY MOUTH WAS ALSO covering my nostrils. I tried to drag in a breath, but no air would come. The man's scar gleamed in the moonlight, exactly as it had in my dreams.

"Shhhhh!" he whispered, bringing his face so close to mine I could count his eyelashes. "You make a noise, and the boys are dead."

His eyes trailed to my left. I turned my head, his hand still smothering me, to see that his friend—the same man Oliver had leveled at the gas station on Friday night—had a nasty semi-automatic trained on Oliver's chest. My vision blurred with tears, and my body started to convulse. Scarface took his hand away and I sucked in oxygen as quietly as possible.

"Now let's go," Scarface whispered.

He grabbed the back of my shirt at the neckline and dragged me out of bed. My bad foot touched the ground, sending a bolt of pain up my leg. I had to bite my tongue to keep from crying out. I cast one desperate look back at Oliver and Marco as Scarface shoved me outside. They were both sleeping soundly. Scarface's thug closed the door with a quiet click and I was flung toward the parking lot.

"Move," Scarface said, drawing out his own gun and pointing it at my feet, one of which I held off the ground.

"Who the hell are you?" I asked through gritted teeth.

"My name is Tomas," he said. "I am a friend of your mother's. Now move, before you lose a toe."

I turned and started limping. The air was cool, but adrenaline was making me sweat even in nothing but my socks, shorts, and T-shirt. Up ahead, his buddy opened the door of a black Audi and got behind the wheel.

"You're no friend of my mother's," I spat, my uncertainty bitter on my tongue. What the hell did I know about my mother? At this point, I would have believed almost anything about her.

The man smirked. "All right, if I'm being truthful, I'm more of a friend of her husband, Hector Tinquera. He is the man who hired me to bring you home to her."

"What?" I asked breathlessly, whirling to face him. "You know where my mother is?"

He snorted. "You don't understand anything, do you? I'm the one who brought her to Hector."

"Wait. Wait!" I shouted as we reached the trunk of his car. His friend got out again, sensing trouble I'm sure, and I balanced on my good leg, stalling as best I could. "Why would you bring me to my mother? She doesn't want to be found."

Scarface's dark eyes flashed, and I knew I'd revealed too much.

"Hector T. wants you dead," Scarface said. "You're the illegitimate daughter from an illegitimate marriage. But he loves his wife, and he thought he might give Marissa one last chance to see you, one last chance to say good-bye—before he slits your throat."

The truth hit me like a punch to the gut, and I choked on my own breath. *This* was why my mother didn't want me to come after her. Because she knew what Hector Tinquera wanted to do to me. She was trying to protect me. And I'd ignored her, playing right into his hands.

Mom. Mom, I'm so sorry.

"Now. Get. In. The. Car."

I pulled back and spat in the man's face as hard and as messily as I could. The man drew a knife on me so quickly I barely had time to flinch before the blade was digging into my stomach.

"Or maybe I will gut you now…"

A shot rang out. Scarface flinched, and then Oliver barreled in out of nowhere, tackling him to the ground with a growl so fierce I couldn't believe it had come from him.

"Oliver!" I screamed.

Scarface kneed Oliver in the gut and Oliver fell sideways onto the asphalt. The man reached for his knife, which had fallen aside on impact, but I gripped the side mirror to keep my balance and kicked it under the car away from him.

"Bitch!" Scarface spat. "You're going to wish you were never born!"

Oliver sprung up behind him. Scarface turned and Oliver backhanded him across the cheek. The man retaliated by slamming Oliver against the next car. He pulled back a fist, and I lunged at him, grabbing his arm, and tried to pull him away from Oliver, but he simply elbowed me in the nose. I heard a crunch, and my vision blurred.

"Kaia!" Oliver shouted, as I went down—hard—on my ass. I pulled my hands away from my face. They were dripping with blood and I couldn't breathe through my nostrils.

"You sonofa—"

Scarface laughed at me, then tilted his head, just in time to see Oliver jump up and pile drive him, crashing an elbow into his jaw from above. Scarface's eyes rolled back in his skull as he fell. His cheek hit the curb between the cars with a sickening crack. His body slumped at an unnatural angle, his neck snapped.

Scarface was dead.

"Oliver!" I pushed my battered body off the ground and flung myself into his arms. He held me so tightly I could feel his ribs pressed against mine.

"I thought you promised never to leave me again," he joked, pushing my hair back from my face. He winced at the sight of all the blood. "Damn. Is it broken?"

"My nose? Who cares about my nose? You saved my life!"

Oliver swallowed hard and looked down at the corpse of the man who had haunted my dreams for a year.

"I owed you one," he said bravely, though I could see the terror in his eyes as the reality sunk in.

"Kids?"

We both looked over the top of the car. Marco was barely holding the half-dead weight of Scarface's driver. Blood poured out of a bullet wound in his chest, near his shoulder.

The gunshot. I'd heard a gunshot right before Oliver had taken Scarface down. Marco must have shot the driver. Behind him, lights were flicking on in some of the motel windows, and an elderly man poked his head out, as if checking to see if the coast was clear.

"We gotta move," Marco said.

Oliver and I locked gazes. I could see the adrenaline overcoming his uncertainty.

"I'll get our stuff," he said.

"I'll help Marco," I replied.

"No." Oliver squeezed my shoulder. "You're half-dressed with a twisted ankle and possibly a broken nose. Get in the backseat and put your foot up. I'll take care of everything."

It was against my nature to let other people do things for me, but for once, I realized I was useless. Blood was dripping all over my shirt, and my ankle felt like every tendon inside of it had been torn free. I opened the car door and crawled into the backseat. There was a sweatshirt on the floor, which I balled up under my nose.

In moments, Oliver was back with our bags and a plastic cup filled with ice. Marco had managed to maneuver

Scarface's partner—whom we were apparently kidnapping—into the front seat. I cast one mournful look out the window at Big Betty and Bettina, hoping that I'd get back to reclaim them before they were stolen or impounded. But even if I didn't, they'd done us proud. And if there was one thing I'd learned from a life on the road, it was not to get attached to material things. I reached up and touched my mom's locket. I had everything that truly mattered in my heart.

Oliver climbed in the backseat and used what looked like a pillowcase to gingerly clean up my nose.

"Ow," I muttered.

He winced. "Sorry."

Marco got behind the wheel and peeled out of the parking lot. I stared at Scarface's limp body as we pulled away. A few motel patrons stood outside their rooms now, and I saw one with a phone to her ear. I just hoped the cops in this town weren't too quick on the uptake.

"I can't even imagine what I look like," I said to Oliver, trying to focus on anything other than what had happened out there.

"You're beautiful," he replied.

Yeah, right, I thought.

Oliver looked out the window. "You're alive," he said. "And that's all that matters."

18 MONTHS AGO

I WRAPPED MY LAST FAKE PASSPORT IN AN OLD T-SHIRT AND SHOVED IT deep into the garbage can inside the airport bathroom in Charleston, South Carolina. Outside, the sky was gray, the air thick with humidity. The cab driver gave me an odd look as I got into the back of his car and rested Sophia across my lap, but I didn't bother to wonder why. Maybe he simply knew sorrow when he saw it.

Outside the window, everything blurred. How was it possible that I was in a world without my parents? Where were they? Was there any chance they were alive? I reached up and touched my mother's locket. I had to hold on to hope. Someday I would see my parents again. I had to believe or I wouldn't survive.

Ten minutes or an hour later, the car pulled up in front of a small, blue house with a big, white porch. In the distance, the Atlantic Ocean rippled in the sun. I shouldered my bag and paid the driver. I stared at the front door. Nothing had ever seemed so foreign to me. This was my new home.

I pushed open the gate and slowly walked up the steps to the porch. The door creaked open before I could knock or ring the bell.

A woman of about sixty with grayish-brown hair and a yellow sweater smiled kindly at me.

"You must be Kaia. I'm Bess."

A man stepped up behind her. He was tall, with a paunch of a belly and a sharp look in his eye.

"This is Henry," she said.

"Hello," he said. I recognized his voice. I'd heard it over the line from the pay phone in Oaxaca.

"Hi," I replied.

"Oh, hon," Bess said. "Welcome home."

She enveloped me in her arms. She smelled of roses and freshly kneaded dough. I hugged her back and tried to feel a connection, tried to feel relief, tried to feel safe.

But the only thing I was, the only thing I'd ever be, was numb.

chapter 31

OLIVER

"PULL OVER HERE," MARCO DEMANDED, AS WE PASSED BY A SIGN for the Joshua Tree National Park. He was sitting in the back seat with Scarface's partner slumped next to him groaning intermittently.

"What? Why?" I asked.

"It's time I interrogate our prisoner here," Marco answered, "before he passes out for good."

I glanced at Kaia, a chill rushing down my arms. Her nose had stopped bleeding, but she'd sprouted yellow bruises under her eyes, which seemed both tired and alarmed. Marco had already explained that we'd taken Scarface's sidekick to keep the authorities off our tails and to get some info out of him about the security at Hector Tinquera's place. What Marco hadn't explained was what he intended to do with the man after he got said information.

This was something I'd spent the last eight hours or so trying not to think about.

I found a parking space as far away from the visitor's center as possible. When I killed the engine, the only sound was the man panting for breath.

"Why don't you two go get him some water?" Marco suggested gruffly. "And take the scenic route."

"What does that mean?" I asked.

"It means give me at least fifteen minutes," Marco snapped. "Now go!"

I shoved open the door and practically fell out onto the hot blacktop. Maybe I was a coward, but I didn't want to know what Marco was about to do, and I definitely didn't want to be around to witness it. Kaia limped around the front of the car and into my waiting arms. I kissed the top of her head and held her, feeling her exhaustion meld with mine. Then we heard the man in the car moan loudly and we pulled apart.

"Are you sure about this?" I asked.

Kaia looked green, but nodded. "We have to know what we're getting into."

There was a thump and a whimper. "No, no! Don't!"

My stomach turned. If I stayed one second longer, I was going to try to stop Marco, which would probably result in a scene, which wouldn't be good for any of us.

"Let's go."

We turned away from the car and, with our arms around each other's backs, walked over to the visitor's center. It looked like a hacienda, with stucco walls and western sculptures, surrounded by cacti and palm trees. Kaia and I navigated the crowds of happy families, keeping our heads down. We caught some curious and disturbed glances, Kaia with her facial bruising and limp, me with her blood down the front of my shirt, but no one held eye contact for long. After grabbing a few bottles of cold water from a vending machine, we wandered back outside and up a slight, dusty slope. The sun was high in the sky, beating down on the desert terrain and the blue mountains in the distance.

Kaia opened one of the water bottles, and sat down on a wide, flat rock. I settled in next to her as she took a sip, then passed me the bottle.

"So…how are you feeling?" she asked.

"Me? What about you?" I looked at her nose and scrunched my own. "That looks like it hurts."

"Only in the most literal sense of the word," she joked, taking the bottle back when I offered it. "But seriously, you…you killed someone. You killed Scarface."

My stomach turned and I looked away, staring at a particularly gnarly cactus a few yards off.

"Yeah, I guess I did." A lump formed in my throat and I quickly swallowed it down. I wasn't sure what I was feeling. Not remorse. Not sympathy. The man was scum, and he'd been trying to kidnap the love of my life. "You saved my life, so I saved yours. Even Stephen."

Kaia looked down at her water bottle.

"That's all you were doing that day in Oaxaca, Kaia," I said. "You were saving your life. And your mom's."

"Yeah, but it turns out I wasn't. It turns out the guys who were after us wanted her alive all along."

"They clearly didn't care that much if they shot the hell out of your room without knowing where you guys were inside of it," I pointed out. I reached for the bottle and took another swig. "This Hector T. guy claims to love your mother? He sure has a funny way of showing it."

Kaia sighed and leaned back on her hands. "This is true. I kind of can't wait to meet the guy."

Something inside me snapped at her casual tone. "You *do* realize how insane this is, right? The guy wants you dead and we're going to...what? Walk up to his front door and ring the bell?"

"No. Hopefully we'll have a better plan once Marco is done with his interrogation."

We both looked off in the direction of our vehicle—Scarface's Audi. It looked so normal there in the parking lot. Like nothing out of the ordinary was going on in the backseat.

"This is crazy. Up until a week ago, I'd never broken a single law in my life," I said, trying to tamp down the tentacles of unease and disgust snaking their way through my chest. "Now I've shoplifted and killed a guy. Also I think we may be aiding and abetting torture, just FYI."

As if she didn't know. But I felt like someone needed to actually say it.

Kaia reached for my hand and squeezed. "It's gonna be okay."

"I really don't see how." I put the bottle aside and drew her hand into my lap. "Forget about everything we've already done; we're going up against a career criminal. What if he hurts you? What if he—"

"Oliver, I know he's a bad guy," Kaia said. "But he has my mother. And I know she's not there because she wants to be. She's being held hostage. That's the only explanation. We have to get her out of there."

I swallowed the lump in my throat. It was fear. No, terror. Terror that this adventure of ours was not going to end well. That this—right here, on this stupid rock with the sun blaring down—might be the last time Kaia and I would ever be alone together.

"I don't want anything to happen to you," I said. "I don't want to lose you. I can't."

"You won't," she said. "Don't give up on me. Please, Oliver. We've come this far. Don't give up on me now."

As hard as it was, I took a deep breath. "Never."

From the corner of my eye, I saw the Audi's door swing open in the parking lot down below. Marco stepped one foot out.

"We could use that water right about now!" he shouted.

"Coming!" Kaia called back.

I got up and reached for her hands, hauling her up onto her one good foot. I expected her to start limping toward the car, but instead, she turned her back on the parking lot and looked out across the beautiful, rocky terrain. I slipped my arm around her back and she leaned into me, her head against my shoulder.

That was when I knew she felt it too, how precious this moment together was.

Another couple strolled by, the girl in short shorts, the guy wearing a UCLA T-shirt. I scanned the license plates in the parking lot, and suddenly, I realized where we were.

"Hey! Check it out!" I said to Kaia. "I took you to California."

Kaia smiled up at me, the sun bathing her face. "Yeah. You totally did."

chapter 32

KAIA

"ARE WE SURE ABOUT THIS?" OLIVER ASKED, GRIPPING MY FINGERS SO tightly they hurt. "Are we absolutely, positively, one hundred percent sure?"

Marco and I exchanged a look.

"No," we said in unison.

And we laughed. Sometimes, laughing is the only thing to do at a life-altering moment like this. Unfortunately, Oliver didn't seem to agree. He rolled his eyes and gritted his teeth. Excitement and fear crowded my heart, and tension pulsated off of him, but I still couldn't help noticing how beautiful he was. Even with a bulletproof vest on and shoulder holsters loaded with automatic weapons.

Okay, especially with a bulletproof vest on and shoulder holsters loaded with automatic weapons. There was something wrong with me. Seriously.

"Look, I don't love the idea of sending my girlfriend off to get her throat slit," he said.

I took a deep breath. Overhead, a pair of black birds

circled, cawing and diving. I told myself they weren't crows. Crows would be a very bad sign.

"That's not going to happen, Oliver. Trust me. Thanks to Scarface's sidekick, we know what we're walking into. Right Marco?"

"Right."

We had dropped our informant at the front door of an emergency room on the outskirts of Los Angeles a little over an hour ago. He'd been unconscious at the time, and we hoped he'd stay that way for a while. Not that any of us expected him to start blabbing about who we were or where we were headed. He couldn't really do that without giving away Hector T.'s whereabouts, and that would be as good as signing his own death warrant. But better safe than sorry.

"This plan better work," Oliver said.

"It will." I leaned in and kissed him, hard and long, on the lips. When we pulled away, I attempted a smile, holding on to hope. "I'm going to go see my mom."

Oliver knit his brow, but he managed to keep it light. "Tell her I said 'hey.'"

I gave Marco a resolute nod, then turned and started to walk, keeping my weight off my bad ankle as best I could. The driveway up to Hector Tinquera's compound was long, winding, and steep, exactly like our thug had said it would be, and I hoped I would make it. How much would it suck if this whole plan went south because I couldn't handle a short hike with my bad ankle?

I watched from the corner of my eye as Marco and Oliver disappeared into the woods and said a silent prayer that Oliver wouldn't get hurt. Maybe I'd find my mom relaxing by the pool, and we'd simply take off into the trees, and no one would be the wiser. We'd meet up with Oliver and Marco at the car, and we'd be done with this whole psychotic episode.

A girl could dream.

The walk took about ten minutes and then, finally, I saw the front gate. Which was a stroke of luck, because my ankle had taken all the abuse it could. The gate was tall and ornate with a big, gold T at its center. I spotted the buzzer to the left of the driveway. I was about fifty feet away when there was a loud clang, and the gates swung open.

I spotted the security camera, which was trained on my face, and gave it a long, hard stare. It wasn't necessary. Clearly, whoever was operating the gate was expecting me. Clearly, they knew who I was.

Once inside, the gates closed behind me, and I found myself facing the front of a sprawling stucco mansion. Plush gardens spread out on either side of the wide, paver driveway, which, at its center, had an island featuring a towering statue of an angel, its wings spread as it looked up at the sky. Ironic. I limped slowly around it and paused. Flanking the front door were four armed guards. They each held an automatic rifle across their chest.

I knew they'd be there, but the sight of them almost made me pee my pants.

Mom. I'm here for Mom. I couldn't stop now.

Slowly, carefully, I approached. Not a single one of the guards moved, but they all followed me with their eyes. When I got to the door, I glanced at the man to my left. He had a goatee and a small silver earring, his hair slicked back into a ponytail.

"So, do I ring the bell or what?" I asked, sounding far braver than I felt.

He turned to me with a dead expression. "Mr. and Mrs. Tinquera are expecting you."

He opened the door. Didn't even frisk me. Weird.

Inside was an open-air foyer with a burbling fountain. According to our informant, the door to the right would lead to an indoor pool and a gaming room beyond, plus a mini-theater and an outdoor entertaining space. Straight ahead I'd find a marble entry with hallways leading off to the dining room and kitchen, the guest wing, and the family's wing. The doors to the left led to Hector's private living room with doors to a library, which no one ever used, and an executive office, where Hector spent most of his time.

I choose the doors to the left, which was where our informant said Hector would be, if he was expecting me.

"And he *will* be expecting you," he'd rasped ominously.

I shoved both doors open and found myself inside a cavernous, tile-floored living room, its walls lined with price-less pieces of art. Standing on the other side of the room, in front of the doors that would lead to the unused library, was my mother.

"Mom?"

The word escaped my lips before I even processed what was happening. I saw her breath catch. She looked thin and frail in white silk pants and a green silk top, her dark hair pulled back in a high bun. My mother, the gym rat, clearly hadn't so much as touched a free-weight in months. There was way too much makeup on her face and marble-sized diamonds sparkled in her ears. It was her. It was definitely her. But it wasn't her.

"Kaia," she breathed.

I ran across the room, my vision blurring, and almost tackled her to the floor, the pain in my ankle forgotten. My mother wrapped her arms around me and pressed her trembling lips to my cheek, near my ear. I could feel her shaking as she tried to hold it together. Something moved behind her. A guard, standing in front of the thick, wooden doors. I didn't, at the moment, care. All I could think was:

Mom, mom, mom, mom, mom.

"Good Lord, what have they done to you?" she asked, gently touching my face.

"Me? Look at you. You're half your normal size."

My mother's eyes went grim.

"You never should have come here, Kiki," she whispered.

My heart sank and I pulled back. "We're going to break you out," I whispered back.

"That's the problem," she said, gazing into my eyes. "I don't want to leave."

Footsteps sounded behind me.

"Well, well, well. There you are, Kaia. It's so good to see you again."

I shuddered at the sound of his voice and slowly turned. Hector Tinquera was exactly how I remembered him. Tall, lithe, with close-cropped black hair and a handsome face that was all angles. He wore a dark red shirt that was open at the collar and pressed khakis. He looked every bit the casual millionaire. His smile was so white it was blinding, and a gold and diamond ring glinted on his right pinkie finger.

My mother trembled, just once—a quick, fleeting tremor. And then, I understood. She was dressed like this because he made her dress this way. The makeup, the jewelry, the scrawny arms. He had turned her into the woman—the wife—he wanted her to be. What she'd said to me a moment ago, it was a lie. She knew he was listening.

"I'm going to kill this man," I said under my breath, so only my mother could hear me. I turned to look her full in the face. "I'm going to kill him for what he did to us, and to dad."

"I always wanted a son," Hector said, stepping closer to us. He flicked his eyes over me appraisingly. "But I suppose you'll do."

"Oh, really?" I asked. "Because I heard you were going to slit my throat."

Hector's eyes betrayed his uncertainty, but he recovered quickly. Apparently he was unaware of our encounter with Scarface or that his right hand man was dead.

"I've changed my mind about that. My boys have your

room all ready for you." Hector strolled over to a bar in the far corner and poured himself a drink. "I heard you like pink."

I laughed. "Actually, I hate it. And I'm not going to move in here and pretend I'm your family."

"Oh, but you will," Hector said, taking a sip of dark brown liquid. "Because if you try to leave, I'll put a bullet in your mother's head."

My heart thumped. I looked at my mom. Tiny beads of sweat dotted her upper lip.

"And if *she* trics to leave, I'll put a bullet in yours." Hector shrugged. "I try to be fair."

"Hector, please," my mother said, taking a step forward. "You know I'm not going anywhere. There's no need to keep Kaia here too. She's young. She has her whole life ahead of her."

"A life that will be spent here, with us," Hector replied. "Don't worry. After a time, I'm sure we'll be very happy together, like the family we always should have been." He took another sip of his drink, then placed the glass on the bar with a clank and picked up a cell phone from the counter. "In fact, we should call your father, Marissa, no?" He shot my mother an evil smile. "Tell him the whole family's finally back together again?"

My mother began to shake. My coolheaded, clear-minded, always-in-control mother shook. Whatever Hector had threatened in the past, this was clearly her worst nightmare. My grandfather was a source of terror.

"No. Hector, please," she sputtered. "Don't—"

At that moment a shot rang out. The guard at the far side of the room went down. Before I could even take a breath, Marco crashed through the door, spraying glass shards across the tile.

"Hello, Hector," he seethed. "So good to see you again."

chapter 33
OLIVER

I SHOVED THE HEAVY LIBRARY DOOR OPEN AS HARD AS I COULD AND hit something solid. The guard. He was right where our informant had said he would be. He staggered backward and was turning around with his gun when I whacked him across the face with one of my own. He fell to the floor, and Kaia grabbed the gun out of my hand.

"Stay down!" she ordered, training the barrel on him.

He lifted his hands in surrender, but Kaia's mother slipped the second gun out of my holster and shot him in the hip. The man screamed and I turned away.

"He's got another three weapons on him," Kaia's mother explained. "None of Hector's men ever have any intention of staying down."

She handed the gun to Kaia and knelt over the man, pulling a pistol out of an ankle holster, a knife out of another, and a third gun from his waistband, all while he writhed in pain and cursed in her face. She barely seemed to notice.

"Who the hell are you?" Kaia's mother asked, whirling on me.

"I'm Oliver, Kaia's boyfriend. Nice to meet you, ma'am."

"Oh, yeah? Well, you're about to be Kaia's dead boyfriend." She tossed the weapons into the study and shut the door, then shoved my gun in the back of her waistband and turned on Kaia. "What were you thinking, bringing a civilian in here? Do you have any idea who you're dealing with? And what the hell did you do to your hair?"

"Mom, we have about thirty seconds before the rest of Hector's security detail comes busting through that door," Kaia said, gesturing toward the front of the room. "Let's get the hell out of here. Marco!"

We all turned to look for Marco, and when I saw what he was doing, my vision went hazy. On the far side of the room, standing in front of the dead body of a guard, was Kaia's uncle, a seriously large silver pistol trained on Hector Tinquera.

Or, the man I assumed was Hector Tinquera. Hector's hands were in the air, but he didn't look in the least bit intimidated. In fact, he looked amused.

"This must make you feel very good about yourself, eh Marco?" the guy asked. "Holding a gun on the man who took your rightful place in your family? Well done."

"Shut up." Marco's hands shook. "Shut up you bastard. My father has no idea who you really are, what you've done to me, to my sister. Today is the day he's gonna find out. Unfortunately, you won't be around to see it."

Kaia and I exchanged a look. How could we not have seen this coming? Marco resented the crap out of Hector T. And we'd given him the perfect opportunity to get his revenge.

"Marco, come on!" Kaia cried. "Remember the plan!"

"You won't pull the trigger, Piglet," Hector said. "You've never had the stones."

"Don't call me that!" Marco screeched.

"Marco!" Kaia's mother stepped forward and for the first time, Marco took his eyes off Hector, but only for a second. "Marco, I understand why you're upset, but you're going to have to put down the gun."

"Not gonna happen, Marisol. You've spent your whole life taking care of me. Well, now it's my turn to take care of you. This is my way of saying thank you." He looked at her, his eyes filled with tears. "And of saying I'm sorry."

"You have nothing to be sorry for. Look around, Marco. It's over. You've done your job. You've brought Kaia and me back together," she said in a soothing tone. "But we have to get out of here. Now."

Something moved outside the window. I saw a man in a suit lift his weapon with two hands, training it on Marco's head.

"Gun!" I shouted, taking a step forward.

There was a plink, the tinkle of breaking glass. Marco slumped to the ground, Kaia and her mother screamed, and then I saw two black disks slide into the room from under the double doors.

"What the hell…"

The air filled with smoke. There was a crash, then distant gunshots. When I checked to see if Kaia was all right, I couldn't even see her.

chapter 34

KAIA

"OLIVER!" I SHOUTED AT THE TOP OF MY LUNGS. "OLIVER?"

He didn't answer. There were shouts and cries and people everywhere. I could feel movement around me, but I couldn't quite see who was there. Someone brushed by. Someone else stepped on my foot. Shots rang out. I heard a voice cry in pain.

"Oliver! Oliver, where—"

That was when I was tackled to the ground. My face practically exploded in pain. The butterfly bandages across my hairline pulled. I kicked and writhed until my mother's voice stopped me.

"Kiki! ¡Cálmate!"

"Mom?"

I looked back and there she was, flattened on the floor on her stomach, one hand on my good ankle. "We have to get out of here, Kiki," she whispered hoarsely. "Now! Come with me. You're gonna have to crawl."

I could see what she meant. The white gas, whatever it was, hung a few inches off the floor, leaving a semiclear sight line. I could see table legs and chairs, black boots running every which way. And Oliver, a good six feet from me, groaning and coughing on the floor. How had he gotten so far away? Was he badly hurt?

"Kaia, come *on!*" my mother whispered, grabbing my hand as she attempted to drag me toward the door.

"Mom, no! Not without Oliver. Not without Marco."

"Marco is dead!" my mother shouted, angry tears cracking her voice. "We have to go!"

"No!" My stomach lurched and I suddenly couldn't breathe. This was not happening. I yanked my hand out of her grip. A man's voice shouted, "Spread out! Spread out!" More shots. Something shattered, peppering the floor with shards of ceramic. I covered my head with my hands and stared desperately at my mother.

"Shit. They're military."

"What?" I blurted.

More shots. *Thunk! Thunk! Thunk!* My mother and I covered the backs of our heads as dirt from a planter rained down around us. Oliver's eyes fluttered.

"Mom, please! I need him."

"Oh for the love of God!" My mother clenched her jaw. "Fine! I'll get him. Just go!"

The smoke began to thin. Oliver rolled over and sat up, blinking, the heel of his hand to his forehead. My mother crawled for him, like a soldier crawling through the muck of battle.

"Stay down!" she directed.

But he either didn't hear her or didn't know she was talking to him. He braced one hand on a couch cushion and pushed himself to standing. The cloud started to thin as Oliver wavered on his feet. And then, like a specter ripped directly from my most horrific nightmares, Hector Tinquera rose up from behind a desk and trained a gun at Oliver's back.

12 MONTHS AGO

I HAD NEVER BEEN SO TIRED IN MY LIFE. I WAS SO TIRED I WAS SHAKING. So tired the skin around my eyes felt tight, my eyes themselves like cotton balls. I needed one good night's sleep. One night without dreams of Scarface and the Handsome Man. One night of not being haunted by images of my mother bleeding on the floor, a boy I'd never known taking his last breaths, my father being shot or stabbed or worse.

But I was never going to get a night like that. It had already been six months without one.

I staggered to my locker, ignoring the questioning stares of my classmates. Somehow I had made it through the first four periods of the day, and it was time for lunch. Another midday meal spent alone under a tree in the yard. That was fine by me. With any luck I'd nod off. Sometimes daytime sleep was dreamless. A half hour of pure nothing. I could deal with a little nothing.

My fingers trembled as I tried to work my lock and got the combination wrong once, then twice. For the third attempt, I rested my forehead against the cool metal, and when I yanked up on the handle, it actually moved. The force jolted the books in my arms and they fell. The heavy one, my chemistry textbook, landed squarely on my little toe.

Hot tears sprang to my tired eyes, but I bit them back. That was when the soccer ball hit me in the shoulder, and I knew the universe had something against me.

"Oh, hey. Need a little help?"

Boy did I ever need a little help.

Someone knelt down beside me. All I could see was a shaggy head of blond hair, a purple and blue bruise on a forearm, a pair of brown work boots. My dad had a pair just like them.

The boy looked up, and our gazes met. His blue eyes were bright until they focused on me, and then they softened. He stood up, holding my books in both hands.

He didn't ask me if I was okay, because clearly I wasn't. But he gave me this smile. This sympathetic, understanding smile and said, "Hey, it's gonna be okay."

"Is it?" I asked.

"I'm Oliver," he said, shifting my books to one arm so we could shake.

"Kaia," I replied.

When I took his hand and he held mine, I knew.

Nothing would ever be the same.

chapter 35

KAIA

"OLIVER!" I SHOUTED.

I grabbed a gun off the floor and aimed it at Hector's heart. My arms had never been so steady. No one was taking Oliver away from me. No one.

My finger squeezed the trigger. The bullet lodged in Hector's shoulder. He turned toward me, his face twisted in anger, and his gun swung around with him. I was about to squeeze off another shot, when blood exploded from Hector Tinquera's chest. The man seemed suspended for half a second, wavering, before he suddenly went down, sprawling like a rag doll across the cherry wood desk.

Oliver stared at me, stunned, alive. Someone else had shot Hector.

My mother rushed to my side. We both turned to see my father stepping into the room in full riot gear, the faceplate on his helmet flipped up. His blond hair was longer, grazing his chin, and his skin was absurdly pale, except for the sunburn across his nose. There was a new scar on his neck—a curved, pink line—but otherwise, he looked exactly the same as the last time I'd seen him.

"Sorry, kiddo," he said with a smile, and chucked his chin at Tinquera's body. "That one was mine."

"David?" my mother breathed, her chin trembling.

"Dad?" I choked out.

He pulled off his helmet, let it drop to the floor, and gathered us both into his arms, kissing us each on the forehead.

"Finally," he said. "We're finally home."

chapter 36

OLIVER

Kaia's family was back together again. I couldn't imagine how that must feel, but considering the fact that she hadn't stopped moving—pacing, bouncing her foot, fiddling with her hair—since we'd all been dropped off at this FBI safe house or whatever, she didn't seem content.

I sat at a small, round table near the wall while Kaia walked back and forth in front of the couch and her mom watched her warily from the corner. The door opened, and all three of us flinched, but it was only Kaia's dad. He'd changed into a clean white T-shirt and jeans, his hair pulled back in a low ponytail. The tattoo on the back of his neck wasn't his only one. He had cursive writing on one arm, military symbols on the other. He wasn't a big guy, but he was clearly powerful. His presence filled the room.

"So…" he began, pressing his palms against his thighs.

"Where have you been?" Kaia demanded.

"It's a long story."

"I can't believe you're really alive," Kaia's mother said, holding her fingertips against her own lips.

She had been clutching one arm around her waist since we left Hector T.'s house in a silver SUV over an hour ago. After a year in captivity, she'd gotten her husband and daughter back and watched the brother she'd risked everything for die. But somehow, she was keeping it together. Like mother, like daughter, I guess.

"Yeah, neither can I to be honest. I'm just so glad the two of you are okay." He took a step toward Kaia and she took a step back. She looked so confused and fragile. I wanted to hold her hand or put my arm around her or *something*, but I felt like I belonged where I was. On the sidelines.

"Tell me where you've been. What happened in Oaxaca? Why did you tell us to run?" Kaia asked, hugging herself tightly.

Her dad blew out a sigh and sat on the edge of the coffee table. Kaia and her mom remained standing.

"I was about half a mile from the motel that day, on my way to scout the job, when the CIA intercepted me," he said, glancing at Kaia's mom. "They told me they had a mission that required my special…talents."

Kaia's expression tightened. Her mom whispered something under their breath.

"I told them no way. I was out. I'd been out for years," Kaia's dad continued. "But they disagreed. They blackmailed me."

He paused and rubbed his forehead, pushing some renegade hairs away from his eyes. "They told me who you really were, Elena. Who your dad was. Your…husband."

"David, I—"

"It's okay," he held up a hand. "We can talk about all that later. The point is, they told me that the Black Death cartel already knew we were in Oaxaca. They said that if I went with them, they'd send someone to protect you two. But if not, you were on your own."

"How the hell did my father find out we were in Oaxaca?" Kaia's mom demanded. "We used assumed names, our Austrian passports."

"Honestly, I think the CIA told the cartel so that the agency could have something over me," Kaia's dad said. "How the CIA found out about your real identity, I still don't know."

"Sonofabitch bastards," Kaia's mom bit out.

"So you said yes? Without a second thought?" Kaia asked.

"No. Are you kidding? You know me," her dad replied. "I tried to fight my way out. Even took out five of their guys before they subdued me." He looked pretty proud of himself. "But there were too many of them and only one of me. I managed to get one of their cell phones and text you in the confusion."

"So what the hell happened?" Kaia demanded. "If you went with them, where was this so-called protection?"

Her dad's eyes darkened. "They were too late. They told me later what had happened. They found the hotel all shot up with no bodies left behind. For the longest time I thought you were both dead. They all did."

I swallowed hard as tears shone in his eyes.

"I went into a depression, I think. I couldn't think straight, so I...I did what they asked. I didn't have anything to live for anyway, so what the hell? I went to Jordan to do another job for the CIA, but things went sideways," Kaia's dad continued. "The intel was bad, and I was captured by the guy I was sent to take out. He and his men held me for almost a year until the government finally sent in a SEAL team. I only got back to the States a couple weeks ago, but I was in a coma for a few days. Let's just say my captors weren't very hospitable."

Kaia's mother walked over to him and knelt at his side. "Oh, David."

"It's okay. Really. I'm fine now," he said, grasping her hand. "But I had a lot of time to think…and to regret decisions I'd made. Like why the hell hadn't I asked the CIA to find out exactly what had happened to the two of you before I went to Jordan? I'd simply accepted what they said—assumed they were right. I was not myself, that's my only explanation. So when I woke up after my rescue, the first thing I did was ask them to find out what had happened to you both. I told them to go to Henry and Bess's place, because I knew that's where you'd be, Kaia, if you were still alive."

"But they didn't send anyone," Kaia said.

"They did, they…" He paused, rubbing his face with both hands before standing and taking her mom with him. "It turned out there was a mole in the room. This guy got a hold of my phone somehow. He sent around a photo of you and put it out there that I was alive and let the world know the locations of all our safe houses, including where you were in Charleston. Basically every asshole who ever felt wronged by us was sent after you."

"Including Hector Tinquera," I said under my breath.

"Exactly," Kaia's dad said.

Kaia sighed. "So that explains Picklebreath." She looked at me. "And the chick in the freezer."

Her dad and mom exchanged a look, but didn't ask her to explain. "Apparently the NSA sent some agents to retrieve you and found an unconscious German patriot on the floor of the house, half a gallon of blood in the kitchen, and you running out the back door," he said. "They chased you, but it seems we trained you right, and you got away."

"So…wait? The black SUV…those were good guys?" I asked.

"One of the black SUVs, at least," Kaia reminded me. "Probably not the one that was shooting at us."

"No, that was the DeCosta brothers." Kaia's dad looked at her mom, who paled. "They are not happy people. The NSA nabbed them instead of you, and you know the rest."

"So we were like five seconds from being rescued," I said, and they all looked at me. "Just to be clear."

"And Henry and Bess?" Kaia asked.

"They found them a half mile from the house. The German apparently tortured them pretty badly, but Bess is gonna be okay." Kaia's dad looked at her mom. "Henry didn't make it."

"Ohmygod." Kaia let out a small sob. Her mom's eyes filled with tears.

"I'm really sorry," I said. "They were always really nice to me."

Kaia's father looked my way. "Listen, Oliver… I want to

thank you for sticking by my daughter. Whatever you two have been through out there, I'm glad she didn't have to go through it alone."

He offered his hand, and I got up to shake it, surprised by how wobbly my knees were. His grip was so strong it was hard for me to match it, but I tried.

"How did you find us, anyway?" I asked.

"A camera at the Joshua Tree National Park rest area got you guys on tape and facial recognition caught Kaia, and then Marco when he went inside. Once they realized you were all together, they tapped into Marco's cell phone and read his texts. That's how we found out where you were headed—where Hector Tinquera lived."

He shook his head, seeming overwhelmed, and looked at Kaia. "I'm so sorry I left you, kiddo. I'm so sorry for everything this last year. I swear to you, if I could have gotten to you sooner, I would have. I'm so, so sorry."

Tears spilled onto Kaia's face, and she took three steps forward, then into her dad's arms. He held onto her as she cried, and he gently rubbed her back. I watched them for half a second before I had to turn away.

I was happy for her. I was. But the jealousy that ripped through me was almost more than I could take. Before anyone could see my tears, I headed out the back door.

chapter 37

KAIA

I WANTED TO GO AFTER OLIVER. CLEARLY, HE NEEDED ME. BUT there was one thing I had to know first. I extricated myself from my father's arms and looked at my mother.

"Have you been here, in the States, this whole time?"

She nodded. My mother never cried, but this was the closest I'd ever seen her come. Her face was almost purple from the effort of containing her emotion.

"Why didn't you get in touch with me?" I asked. "Why didn't you at least let me know you were alive? Do you have any idea what this year has been like for me?"

"I was trying to protect you, Kiki," my mother said, the lines at the corners of her eyes deeper and sadder than I remembered. "Hector…he had someone watching me at every moment. He knew my every move. He was constantly threatening to track you down and…" She paused and swallowed a few times before continuing. "I had to do what he said…say what he wanted me to say…or he would have come after you."

"Why didn't he kill me in Mexico?" I asked.

My mom's gaze darted to my dad, then back to me. "He was about to. He knocked you out, but when he raised a gun to you, I grabbed your pistol and put it to my head. I told him if he killed you, I'd kill myself, and then he'd never get what he wanted."

Sounded familiar.

"Jesus, Elena," my father said.

"Well it worked, didn't it?" she countered. "She's alive." Her fingers raked at the skin at the base of her neck, and I realized suddenly it was her nervous tick. She used to play with her locket, which was now around my neck, so there was nothing there for her to touch. "You should know something, Kiki. Oaxaca was supposed to be our last job."

I blinked. "What?"

"It was a massive payday. Enough for us to retire," my father said. "We knew how much you wanted out and we wanted you to have a normal life. What we'd been doing to you…dragging you all over the world, never giving you time to make friends, go to school, have birthday parties… It was wrong. It was—"

"Selfish," my mother interjected.

"So when we got back, we were done."

I sat down hard on a chair. All these missed chances. Everything could have been so different. I felt like crying for what my life could have been, but I was all dried out. No tears would come.

"So how did you send that text to me? Telling me to stay away?" I asked. "I mean, if you were being watched."

My mother cleared her throat and glanced at my father. He gave her a supportive nod and somehow, that made me feel more solid too. Obviously, they'd been through hell. They'd been ripped apart, not knowing whether I was alive, whether they'd ever see each other again. My mother's lies had been revealed to my father. My mother had spent the past year married to an evil man. But still, they were managing to be there for one another now. We were going to be okay.

"I was allowed one half hour each day, most days anyway, to bathe on my own," my mother began. "A few days ago, I overheard Hector and Tomas talking about your father. I couldn't hear everything, but I caught enough to make me believe he might be alive. So I lifted one of the guards' personal cell phones and smuggled it into the bathroom with me."

She paused and reached for my father's hand. "I used the cell phone to check the safe house cameras for signs of your dad. Instead, I saw you."

"In Chicago," I said.

"Yes, in Chicago." She gave me a wan smile.

"Hector would have killed you if he'd found out you stole that phone," my father said.

"Yes, but he would have killed the guard if he'd ever reported his phone missing, so I took the risk that the man wanted to live."

My father nodded, proud of her logic. She blushed.

"A couple of nights ago, Hector told me he'd sent Tomas after you, Kaia. He said now that he knew David was alive he wanted to kill you himself. He wanted to take away the most precious thing in David's life, like David had taken his."

"I'm so glad I put that bastard down," my father said.

"I'm so sorry, Kiki. About everything." My mother reached for my hand, and I let her take it. "But the important thing is, we're back together now. All of us."

"I'm sorry about Marco," I told her, my voice thick. "He was so worried about putting me and Oliver in danger. I never thought about the fact that I was putting him in danger."

"He loved you, kid," my mother said, sounding so much like Marco it was painful. "If he had a choice, he would have rather you walked out of there alive than him."

Hot tears fell onto my cheeks. My mom reached for my dad, and he pulled us both into another hug. I let myself drink them in for a moment, inhaling them, memorizing their feel, before I pulled away.

"So…what're we gonna do?" I asked, drying my tender, bruised face with my fingertips.

"What do you mean?" my mother asked. She reached out to touch her locket, which lay flat against my chest, and smiled.

"Where are we going to go?" I asked, looking at my father. "Are you back in the CIA for real? Are we always going to be stalked by this army of hit men your mole sent after me? Are we going to have to keep moving?"

My mother and father exchanged a look. Clearly, neither of them had thought that far ahead.

"I never thought I'd get out of that prison," my mom said.

"I was pretty much focused on getting you both safe," my dad replied.

"Well then, maybe you two should talk."

I took a step back. I'd done enough heavy thinking for one week. It was up to them now. They were, after all, the parents. I headed out the back door after Oliver, but paused on the threshold.

"One thing," I said. "If we do get a new house, no pink in my room."

chapter 38

OLIVER

A TINY YELLOW AND BLACK BIRD FLEW FROM ONE PALM TREE TO another on the enclosed back patio, chasing after its mate. I'd been watching their game for five minutes and kept rooting for the little guy to catch up, but he never did. When Kaia opened the door behind me, the two birds took off into the sky.

I was so nervous I felt sick. Kaia walked around the picnic table and climbed up to sit next to me on the tabletop. I looked down at our matching black boots, covered in the dirt and grime from four days on the road. I kind of wanted to take a picture of them.

Kaia lifted my arm and draped it around her. I pulled her in close.

"I love you, you know," she said.

"Yeah, I do." It was hard to keep my voice from cracking, but I managed. "I love you too." I kissed her temple and sighed. "So what now?"

"Apparently, no one has figured that one out," she said. "But I do know one thing." She lifted her head to look me in the eye. "You are not going back to that house."

My breath caught. "You mean Robin's? What about Trevor?"

"It's not your responsibility to worry about Trevor," she told me. "It's his mom's."

"I know, but—"

"Oliver, you can't go back there," she said firmly.

And even though I knew it was true, even though I'd wanted nothing more than to get away, it felt wrong somehow.

"But I can't just leave him," I said. "I have to at least do something to help him."

She considered, her brow knitting. "Maybe my dad can get someone to go over there and help them," she said. "He does have a lot of government connections, and from what I can tell, they owe him big time at this point."

"You think? And maybe they can tell Robin I'm okay? I mean, assuming she cares." I said. "Would you really talk to your dad about it?"

"Of course." Kaia smiled. "I'm sure he'll figure something out. I know I don't look like a spoiled brat, but he's pretty much never said no to me in my life."

"I think that was clear from the motorcycle. And the iPad. And the absurd number of ceramic unicorns in your bedroom."

"Which we will never speak of again," she said, raising her eyebrows in warning.

"Oh, I have so much dirt on you now," I joked. "I know you drool in your sleep… I know you hum Elmo songs… I know your dad is a superhero geek…"

She shut me up with a kiss and when she went to pull

away, I held her to me. I didn't know how many more of these we were going to get. I had to make the most of them.

"So…what about your family?" I asked, when we finally parted. It was the hardest question to ask, but I had to ask it. "Do you think you'll go back to Houston?"

Kaia sighed and took my hand, entwining our fingers and holding them atop her thigh.

"I don't know. I don't even want to think about it. Which is funny, because it used to be the only thing I ever thought about." She shook her hair behind her shoulders and smiled. "I say, we live in the now."

"How do we do that, exactly?" I asked, a little flutter of excitement inside my heart.

"We're in California, right?"

I grinned. "Yeah, we are."

"Well, I've still never seen the Pacific Ocean," she reminded me.

"From this side, anyway," I finished.

She jumped down onto the flagstone patio, tugged me from the table, and we were off.

chapter 39

KAIA

My parents weren't about to let me out of their sight, but at least they kept their distance, hanging back on the boardwalk while Oliver and I dug our toes into the sand. There were half a dozen CIA agents around too, watching over us, protecting us from whatever unknown threats were still out there—but I tried not to think about that. Oliver, standing in the pink light as the sun went down, was too beautiful to allow me thoughts of anyone else.

"I could get used to this," he said, dropping to grab a handful of sand and letting it slowly slip through his fingers as he straightened up again.

"Best afternoon adventure ever," I said, and he laughed. "Plus, it is *so* much prettier from this side."

Oliver turned me toward him and looked into my eyes. He slipped his warm hands along my cheeks and held my face.

"It's over," he said. "How does it feel?"

I glanced over my shoulder. My parents held each other on the other side of the guardrail, yards and yards away, kissing like it was their first time. Gross. But also, awesome.

"It feels good," I said. "I actually feel…peaceful."

Oliver smiled wistfully, maybe a little sadly, then leaned in for our own first-time-like kiss. When we parted, he was smiling for real.

"When I was a kid and my mom would take me to the beach, she'd always race me to the water and let me win."

"Aw! That's so cute," I said squeezing his hand.

"You up for it?" he challenged.

I blinked. "Um, I think we've done enough running for one lifetime. And also…"

I lifted my foot to show him my ACE Bandage.

"Right. Sorry. From now on, no more running."

"A stroll then?" I suggested with a smile.

He grinned back. "I'll take it."

<hr />

The wind tossed our hair back from our faces as the sun dipped below the water's edge. There was so much turmoil behind us, but all that was in front of us was the endless ocean and a million possibilities.

I took Oliver's hand, and we walked, very slowly, to the water's edge.

ACKNOWLEDGMENTS

Thank you so much to my bafflingly tireless agent Sarah Burnes, who champions everything I do, and to Aubrey Poole, who first saw the potential in Kaia's story. Special thanks also go out to Annette Pollert-Morgan, who made an already cinematic story read like a blockbuster, and to Cassie Gutman and Katelyn Hunter, for their incredible eye for detail. Heartfelt thanks to Jason Richman, whose enthusiasm for this book made it all seem worthwhile.

I couldn't have written about motorcycles with anything approaching accuracy without the help of my brother, Ian Scott, and my old friend Joe Mandile, so thanks for your input, you guys! And, as always, I have to thank my mom—gone from this world, but present in every tap of the keyboard—my sister, Erin, and the three loves of my life—Matt, Brady, and William.

Thank you to my author support group—Jen Calonita, Elizabeth Eulberg, and Jen Smith. Where would I be without you guys to vent to and laugh with? (Answer: curled in a ball in the corner.)

To all the librarians, booksellers, bloggers, reviewers, and fans who continue to support my books, thank you, thank you, thank you for continuing to give me a reason to write. You occupy a huge space in my heart.

Lastly, thanks to Chris Hemsworth, who appeared in my dream one night (G-rated, people! Get your minds out of the gutter!) and inspired this story.

ABOUT THE AUTHOR

Kieran Scott is the author of several acclaimed young adult novels, including the Non-Blonde Cheerleader trilogy, the He's So/She's So trilogy, the True Love trilogy, and *Geek Magnet*. She is a senior editor at Disney/Hyperion and resides in New Jersey with her family. Visit kieranscott.net.